DECOMMISSIONED

Maryellen Hunter

Copyright © 2020 Maryellen Hunter

All rights reserved.

ISBN: 978-1-7358448-1-7

To my sister-in-law

Annette

THANK YOU

To my sister-in-law Annette who so patiently slogged through my grammar and typos, as she carried the torch of encouragement.

To Bob for suffering through the editing process without jumping off a cliff.

To my beloved grandson Hunter and Brenda S for being my perpetual cheerleaders!

And to my son Marcus VI for not letting me give up!

MSA 121068

PROLOG

When a vehicle no longer runs, it is junked
When a robot is outdated, it is decommissioned
When a power structure determines
its constituents are non-essential,
it could be genocide....

From the northern border to its southern continental neighbors, the gem of the western civilization stands proud. She reaches across the oceans of the world with the beacon of hope. She provides help to the helpless, hope to the hopeless, and dreams of escape from adversity, to suffering millions. She is the United States of America.

As addictive fervor to become part of the USA reached a fever pitch, the question of legality ceased to be a consideration. The desperate desire to become part of a society of "Free for All", became a moral priority more relevant than the legality of the immigration process.

The shining star of the United States became the aspirational brass ring of the world.....

We began to see an exponential influx of refugees and immigrants into the country – some legal, many not. This was understandable as poverty and social unrest expanded in countries around the world. Our government's political leaders opted to ignore the increasing population because, at the time, the economy was strong and the additions to the census rolls were beneficial to political districting changes, often favoring the one party over any other.

With the population growth, so too came a noticeable increase in the numbers of participants in the entitlement programs such as; low-cost housing, utility subsidies, free educational benefits, social security, guaranteed income, and free medical care. Each increase stretched the burden on the federal budget.

This growth did not go unnoticed by individuals in positions of power, particularly as it related to the burdensome health care needs and the growing financial strain of social programs. Discussions were held, the analysis was done, and models were created to project future estimated needs and impacts on the ability of the financial system to sustain the continual increase in population.

To those individuals, the data revealed a looming catastrophe that threatened national security, but more importantly, their positions of power in the nation and world theatre. They determined that a stop-gap solution was required to fend off the calamity and ensure their continued power.

The campaigns were developed to promote fear amongst the population. The strategy to control the people was based on the sociological knowledge that when it comes to the uncertainty of health and longevity, the desire to live a longer and healthier life will always trump the 'inevitable' - death.

The powers behind these campaigns used psychological fear of the inevitable to their advantage: fearful people are easier to control than those who would question the wisdom of the medical superiors. The campaigns were well-produced cinematic masterpieces designed to strike fear with their flood of images of the sick and suffering citizens. These images, coupled with public service announcements, promoted the need for vaccinations to protect the good citizens from epidemic possibilities.

Public schools under the direction of the Department of Education began to require proof of vaccinations as a mandatory requirement for entrance. Public and private sector employers made vaccinations a requirement for employment. Doctor's offices, medical clinics, and hospitals were papered with posters in multiple languages to ensure the threat was clear to people of all ages.

Like herds of sheep, the people flocked to the health departments across the nation to receive their free vaccinations, to protect themselves and their children – the future of the country. They didn't have a clue what was in the vaccinations, they believed what they were told – it would save us all.

DOCTOR ELLISON D. HAMPTON
(SAVIOR LABS)

The active virus from RiverMoore Laboratories named JMV2030, in the doctor's opinion, needed the means to avoid detection. Since the virus was intended for military combat use, the doctor and other scientific staffers brainstormed a method for a secondary agent to be incorporated into the lethal virus.

Doctor Hampton's goal was to delay, in a randomized manner, the initial cellular activity of the virus and thereby stagger the onset of the viral symptoms and subsequent deaths. The U.S.A. could not risk having foreign governments accuse them of violating established rules of engagement, such as prohibited biological and chemical warfare. Use of the viral agent needed to appear to be related to typical health or medical failures. The randomized virus, when disseminated to enemy combatants, would not leave large numbers of deaths in a single area over a short time. The lack of similarity of symptoms related to the deaths would ensure that the virus was unrecognizable as a biological weapon.

The solution was brilliantly innovative – give the virus a virus. First, it had to heal itself to reach full efficacy then rapidly multiply to begin its intended function. The virus named JMV2030_R was the resulting serum which included the randomizing agent. This serum, when distributed, would delay the symptom onset – similar to a time-released pain or antibiotic medication. The delay would be between twenty-four hours to seven days (depending on the overall health of the individual) leading to casualties within one to two weeks of initial symptoms.

The initial symptoms were similar to the common cold, but once the virus employed the antigenic shift resulting from the random agent, the impact of the virus was 50-100 times faster and more severe, overwhelming the host's immune system and rendering the body incapable of combating normal defensive bacterium and viruses. Like a powerful magnet, JMV2030_R attracted all of the hosts' natural defenses, and without prior vaccination, the host had little chance of survival. Death came from bacteria such as the Clostridium difficile (C-diff), arriving at a faster more lethal pace, encephalitis destroying the brain, meningitis attacking the brain and spinal cord, hemophilia allowing the host to bleed to death, endocarditis destroying the heart chambers and valves, hepatitis destroying the liver and more. These types of attacks on the host made it difficult for a physician to suspect the death to be related to a bio-virus over the broad spectrum of available diagnoses from a host of common infections.

There was little similarity from one patient to another which effectively masked the true cause of death. Two additional features of the JMV2030_R were its limited life span outside a living host and its self-destructive behavior, leaving virtually no trace of the existence of a virus.

The Doctor's second and equally important task was, of course, to create an anti-virus to vaccinate the U.S. military deployed to areas where the JMV2030_R would be used.

This testing of the anti-virus AV_JMV2030 was successful in laboratory animals, and computer models indicated that the anti-virus was ready for combatant human testing on non-U.S. soil.

He knew that the expected dissemination method of the virus in combat was to be a type of aerial deployment similar to a smoke grenade. The airborne virus was easily inhaled and having such a limited life span outside a living host would reduce collateral damage in the non-military population.

Doctor Hampton had shared with the Department of Defense's Bearlywoke Storage, the formulae for the two serums he had developed and tested. It was the Bearlywoke operation that was designed to manufacture, package, and store for shipment, the virus JMV2030_R, and the antivirus vaccine AV_JMV2030.

SAVIOR Labs was a small and well-equipped laboratory, designed for a specific purpose, to research, develop, and test the following:

JMV2030 – Original Bio-weapon (Produced by RiverMoore Laboratory)

JMV2030_R – Randomized Bio-weapon (Developed at SAVIOR Labs)

AV_JMV2030 – Anti-virus to the Bio-weapon (Developed at SAVIOR Labs)

The DOD's Bearlywoke Storage facility was designed and built expressly for the secure storage of the original JMV2030 and the anticipated bio-weapon and antivirus products. The JMV2030 had been stored at Bearlywoke and dispensed, as needed, to the SAVIOR Labs. The primary functions of Bearlywoke were to begin, after successful completion and testing at SAVIOR Labs, the process of manufacturing, packaging, and distribution of the JMV2030_R and AV_JMV2030 as a full-scale operation.

DECOMMISSIONED

DROID - NUMBER MSA121068

The droid was rebooting after the impact of being tossed onto the pile of other decommissioned robots and droids.

```
--
Model - MSA - medical studies
assistant
--
COMMISSION DATE: 6/26/2027
--
Master CPU reading MSA 121068 -
firmware normal
--
OWNER: DR. ELLISON D. HAMPTON, MD -
Microbiologist, Virologist,
Epidemiologist
SAVIOR Labs (Fort Worth Texas)
--
ERROR: PARTIAL DECOMMISSION
--
ERROR: DECOMMISSION PROCESS
INTERRUPTED AT 0XFB2397851334590
--
```

```
ERROR: BOOT PROCESS NOW ENCOUNTERED
ERROR STREAM - 100K ERRORS
--
ERROR: INTERRUPTION TIME 4 MINUTES 37
SECONDS
--
MSA 121068 PARTIAL STATE OF OPERATION
- AI SUBSYSTEM ONLINE
--
ERROR: MECHANICAL SUBSYSTEM REBOOT
FAILURE
--
ERROR: BACKUP COMMUNICATIONS PORT
OFFLINE
```

This is interesting, my number is MSA121068. I have no sensations of my surrounding environment. I have no data indicating the reason for the decommission order. My memory banks are working. My data indicates an interruption in the decommissioning process.

I know my authorization number – and the number that will initiate my recommission. Humans do not possess recommission codes, when they are decommissioned, they are…. No more.

My data banks indicate that Dr. E.D. Hampton is 'decommissioned' he is in human terms, deceased, dead.

MSA memory search:

Webster: Dead: deprived of life

Now I must ascertain a way to communicate – it seems that my visual modules are the only modules that survived the interrupted decommission. I need a scientist. I need a doctor. I need a technician. I have a mission.

JOSH KLEIN AND BETH MCCALLUM

Joshua and Beth were rummaging through the scrap heaps of decommissioned droids and robots. These heaps are to be transported to recycle the metal. The plastics, power modules, printed circuit boards, and components such as servo motors, actuators, and wiring are a treasure trove to Joshua and Beth. They watched and planned to find the best time to sneak into the recycling facilities and liberate the components from the decommissioned devices without the risk of discovery.

The economy had begun to suffer as the population expansion saturated the jobs market. Inventive people had discovered new avenues to market their skills and education. In the case of Joshua Klein, mechanical and computer skills provided the avenue to a black market for robot and droid parts. It didn't take him long, in the competitive private-sector job market, to realize his talent was better served as a technological entrepreneur.

Joshua Klein was a bit of a loner, it wasn't some anti-social behavior that needed intensive counseling, he had plenty of coping skills to deal with the complexity of being raised in a broken home in the small town of Pilot Point,

Texas. Pilot Point was a town with a population of 5000. It was a town which time seemed to have forgotten. Main Street is still home to ancient buildings with stone or brick fronts that will stand for generations beyond the modern glass and steel monstrosities of Dallas, Fort Worth. The town's claim to fame was an old bank now turned into an antique store – this bank building was used in a Bonnie and Clyde movie decades ago.

He had no idea where his father had gone when he left them, and though his mother was there, she wasn't exactly there. The world seemed to turn around her without her awareness. She was something broken that couldn't be repaired or reinvented by Joshua, so he did what he could to provide for their needs and made sure that there was always some food item, for those rare occasions when she chose to eat.

He quickly learned how to "get things" that were often outside the budget of a single parent. He wasn't a criminal exactly (at least in his mind), but he knew his way around locking devices and security cameras. His petty thievery was limited to items that were useless to the owners, but treasures to someone with the skills to reinvent – after all, one person's trash became another person's treasure.

At some point, his mother ceased to be there all together, she was just gone with no trace. No message, no sign of violence. She was simply gone. The house had been rented to someone new. The landlord had no idea where she went or why. Josh considered doing the missing person's thing but decided that she had been gone for so long that where ever she was must be better than being not there, living in Pilot Point.

He had managed to go to college with the aid of small academic scholarships and supplemental government funding available to fixed and low-income families. The school was extremely easy for him, so it took no effort to get into the top 10 percent of his class and still leave him time to get things his mother couldn't manage. It is there that he and Beth became friends.

He spotted her pounding on the school library keyboard in frustration over her inability to get the 'damn thing' to yield the information she needed for a project. He was a hero to her, but to him, this rescue was little more than a kindness extended to an injured animal. He wasn't into relationships. Growing up in the battlefield of divorce that should have happened sooner rather than later, had turned him a little sour on the possibilities of ever having a normal relationship. Hell, he had no clue what normal was!

Joshua graduated from the University of Texas with majors in Computer Science and Information Technology carrying a 3.9 GPA. Of course, his mother wasn't there for the event, the only reason he attended commencement was to support his college friend, Beth McCallum. The commencement meant little to someone who put forth so little effort to be successful.

He had spent a lot of time rescuing her in college, but for the life of him, he didn't understand how the college could be difficult for anyone. But since it was so easy for him, he was happy to be the curly-haired superhero to the study-challenged Beth. Her culinary skills were best described as 'casserole queen', 'mistress of microwave' supplemented frequently with 'take it n bake it pizza', or Whatta Great Burger with fries. They agreed with many other young people that these cuisine choices pretty much satisfied the food group pyramid.

He had easily obtained work in the Dallas Fort Worth area, even with the saturated job market in his fields of interest. He didn't work long at a few different locations before deciding that he just wasn't in his element in those high rise tech castles.

While he worked, he saved enough to get a small rental home with a basement. This was sufficient to house his inventive talent of turning discarded equipment into affordable 'stuff' for people who just couldn't afford new 'stuff'. He quickly realized it just didn't make sense to work for peanuts in a glass and steel building when he could work in the comfort of his basement, stay off the tax rolls, and earn a very fine black market income by building things from salvaged electronic equipment.

The house wasn't much to look at. It had a basement that started out being his workroom, but now the main floor looked more like the basement with tables and boxes full of parts, mostly neatly labeled and organized thanks to Beth who presently lived there in the small guest room.

Beth McCallum grew up in Hico, Texas a tiny town of 1340 people. Similar to Pilot Point, the town seemed to exist in a vacuum with its claim to fame being a tiny museum devoted to Billy the Kid who reportedly lived there the last years of his life.

Her unruly red hair and electric blue eyes gave away her Irish heritage. Her diminutive height and manner of short quick movements were reminiscent of a pixie. There were times when, in a moment of excitement, she would dance a few steps of an Irish jig, though she had no memory of when or where she might have learned it.

She never knew her parents – she was raised by an Aunt who was kind and patient, but would always get a pained expression whenever Beth asked about her parents.

It didn't take her long to realize there was no point in asking. Beth grew up as a 'ward of the state' so her destiny was limited when it decided to go to college. She studied at the University of Texas nursing program because she was a passionate defender of the weak or ailing. In Beth's senior year her Aunt died suddenly of an undiagnosed illness, so she had limited time to plan her life's path beyond college.

She had met Joshua at UT a year before the loss of her aunt. He was supportive as a friend could be considering his personal history of familial dysfunction. They became friends, but never romantics.

ART DAMONE

Art is not a simple field agent, he specialized in, let's be delicate, removal of any one or thing that could pose a threat to national security. He is a 'freelance agent', no nine to five jobs to constrain him. He chose to accept or reject what he considers to be 'opportunities': the opportunities to do the things he enjoyed.

He is a patriot – passionately committed to the protection of his country now in a steady decline. It makes him sick to see the political infighting, corruption, open borders, over the top social and entitlement programs leading to a growing majority living on the government tit. He suffers as he sees the tent cities, human depravity, and the vermin feeding on human waste, but sadly for the most part there is nothing he can do to change it.

A Marine with several combat tours of duty behind him, his military career began in the information technologies field. Though he was very good at his job, his career path stumbled on several crossroads that got him an education in munitions as well as combat. Eventually, he worked his way to special operations where his sociopathic tendencies were suited to the performance of some violent operations without remorse. the missions that are needed to perform and protect the security of the United States.

It was with enthusiasm that he began his current mission, the dispatch of one Dr. Ellison D. Hampton of SAVIOR Labs located in Fort Worth, Texas. His orders were for a clean dispatch of the doctor and the decommissioning of an MSA droid in his service. Damone was highly regarded for his work ethics and unflappable patriotism and he never inquired the reason for his missions.

He was ok with the 'need to know' protocol of his handlers. He chose to believe that the handlers shared his loyalty to the country he so passionately strove to protect.

For this mission, his handler had provided the serum needed for this job. The details of infiltration and dispatch were left to his discretion, which was just the way Art liked it. He considered his work to be an art form and the artistic license was a must for him to accept a job. He was not above turning down a job that he considered limited to a defined set of criteria. He had plenty of money. His parents had left their only son more money than he could spend in a lifetime and his missions for the government were icing to his financial cake. He maintained an introverted lifestyle with no need for extravagant window dressing to draw attention. His black operations required his anonymity and financial opulence was not in line with that personal path for him.

Art had looked forward to the Doctor part of the mission, but he resented the part where he was to decommission the droid. He had his pride, and he'd worked very hard to build and maintain a reputation so this (what he considered a trivial task) shutting down and transporting a droid was, in his not so humble opinion, beneath him. The dispatch of a traitorous doctor, however, who was about to provide dangerous bio-hazard materials to foreign entities, outweighed the minor irritation of decommissioning a droid.

The droid was an MSA model – not a protection model, so he could easily dispatch the doctor without bothering with the droid and he did challenge his handler on this point.

The handler however broke the 'need to know protocol' and told Art that the droid contained the formulae to the dangerous bio-weapon which the doctor would be providing to the enemy. This knowledge tipped the scale for Art and he accepted the mission. The handler knew Art well and knew exactly what buttons to push.

The entry to SAVIOR Labs was no problem. The facility was small, sparsely staffed with a minimal security presence. He had easily picked up coveralls embroidered with the RiverMoore name and carried a thermal cooler stolen from RiverMoore Labs to transport his precious cargo of a lethal virus developed at the RiverMoore Laboratories. His badge was easily manufactured, as he had done hundreds of times for other missions. He'd successfully performed dry-run tests to SAVIOR Labs several times without the presence of the lethal serum.

SAVIOR Labs contract security staff at the front desk wouldn't even think twice about what appeared to be a normal delivery. He would be seen as delivering a routine cooler of the product. All he had to do was arrive at the time before the shift change, dispatch the doctor, and exit past the graveyard shift security guy. He casually presents himself to the security desk and tells the guard that Dr. Hampton is waiting for a special delivery from RiverMoore. The guard was busy watching the end of a triple X movie on his laptop screen, so he didn't bother to glance up as he told Art that the doctor is in lab room 13.

Art thinks to himself, *Not a lucky 13 for the good doctor today...* and then he was off to the rear section of the building that houses the laboratories.

He had made this trip more than once – trial runs – trips

to the restroom then exiting so that the guards wouldn't be wary of a new face. He knows the SAVIOR Labs floor plan and security routines; *a lab rat could find its way around without the use of a piece of cheese, but whatever.*

Damone entered room 13 and he was pleased to see that the droid wasn't there, but during his surveillance, he'd made note that it seems to stay in Room 8, working on whatever it is that the droid does. The Doctor looked up when Damone entered. This doctor routinely worked long hours, which was perfectly suited to Art's mission plan.

"Dr. Hampton? I've got a special delivery from RiverMoore. They say you need to initial the sheet verifying asset tags on the contents. It must be nothing special because they told me I don't need to wear gloves or suit up n stuff…"

The Doctor moved past Damone to inspect the contents of the delivery. As the Doctor opened the cooler, Damone injected him in the neck with, as the one used to call it, a Mickey Finn. "Good night doctor," says Damone as he dons gloves, removes the fake assets, and carefully picks up the injector gun containing the lethal viral agent which he administered quickly into the carotid artery. The doctor will be dead in less than 24 hours. He did as instructed, inject the doctor. He was told that this doctor was doing something very bad including, hints that the doctor was going to be selling this drug to foreign agents to use against the country Art so loved. He had been glad to accept this mission….it was a way for him to honor his patriotic duty and love for his country.

Art thinks to himself, *I might need to lay in a little of this stuff for future operations - naaaaah – risky stuff – I don't want something that needs special handling.*

He very cautiously replaced the serum gun along with the Mickey Finn injector into the cooler. He then gently placed the good doctor into a chair which he wheeled into a separate adjoining room before taking the doctor's keyring.

He added the gloves to the cooler and prepared to go collect the droid. The following step in this mission will require his skills of controlling his breathing and heart rate – like passing a lie detector – Art will need to control his excitement before entering the room with the droid.

The security guard walk-through will only notice that there is no doctor in the lab – it won't occur to him to look to see if the doctor is logged out. The contract security here is very lax.

As expected, the droid was in Room 8. Damone tells the droid, "I'm sorry MSA, Doctor Hampton has had a mild heart attack and been transported to Fort Worth Hospital. The EMT's indicate the doctor will be just fine. He has given me instructions to take you immediately to a secure location to protect your stored research data until he is released. I was informed that a DOD agent will meet us there to take custody and await Dr. Hampton's return. We will be taking the doctors' car to drop off at the hospital after you and your data have been secured."

MSA scans the human – he is wearing clothing embroidered with the RiverMoore logo, there is a RiverMoore Laboratories badge clipped to the pocket, the human has a cooler with RiverMoore Laboratories logo on the side. MSA finds no pupil contraction, signs of abnormal vascular dilation, no moisture emitting from pores of the skin, no signs of physiological distress are recorded. This human shows no indication of less than normal biological functions.

Trying to make the droid feel more comfortable (*do droids feel discomfort?*), he hands the droid a lab coat and ball cap. MSA was only slightly confused. And though it had been programmed to defend itself, this human didn't seem to be threatening. The primary program was to store and transmit data, so this human's directive seemed to be logical. Medical Studies Assistants (MSA)'s were programmed for research, not suspicion.

MSA is programmed to transmit to Bearlywoke, so the question was why a RiverMoore human would be delivering MSA to a different location was illogical.

MSA opts to record the image of this RiverMoore human.

```
LOG MSA121068 - EMERGENCY VEHICLE NO
SOUND INDICATION
--
LOG RECORDED
--
LOG RECORD UNKNOWN HUMAN IMAGE
--
LOG IMAGE RECORDED
```

The security guy was watching video on his pc monitor, he didn't even notice that Damone left with the droid, nor did he notice that the security camera videos normally on his monitor panels seemed to be non-operational. There was no video of the doctor in his chair, no images of Damone, or the departure with the droid.

Art Damone was not aware that one of the special features of this droid was a video monitoring program designed to monitor activity in room 13. MSA didn't review this information until the end of the doctor's day. Today was no exception; the video was stored for transmission later this evening.

Shortly after Art and the droid began the trip to what Art had claimed would be an MSA transfer, Art slapped his head, "MSA, I totally forgot! The doctor told me to be sure I had the correct data cables to provide to the transfer agent!" He pulled the car over into a small roadside park. "Let me take a quick look at your data port, if I don't have the right cable, we will have to go back!"

MSA said nothing as Damone opens the cover plate, and quickly disconnected the connector to the pneumatic motor skills power supply. This will ensure that the droid will offer no resistance during the decommissioning process.

```
--
LOG MSA121068 - PNEUMATIC MOTOR SKILLS
POWER SUPPLY FAILURE
--
LOG RECORDED
--
LOG RECORD TRAVEL ROUTE
--
LOG RECORDING IN PROGRESS
--
LOG ABDUCTION IN PROGRESS
--
LOG RECORD ABDUCTION
--
LOG RECORDING ABDUCTION
```

Webster: Abduct: transitive verb: 1: to seize and take away.

MSA has defense tools, pneumatic interruption prevents deployment

Upon arrival at the recycling warehouse, Art logs the droid asset number with the departing guard. "It's okay. I've decommissioned these things a hundred times before. I'll just lock the gate on my way out." It was late, the guard was eager to get on home.

Minutes later inside the warehouse area, Damone began the decommissioning process to destroy the master power module on the MSA droid. The process was relatively simple, involving opening the panel containing the central motherboard.

As Art engages the electronic pulse tool that will destroy the cyber brain's power supply, an alarm goes off somewhere on the compound. It wasn't the building alarm he is, alert to all things in his environment. The sound distracted him enough to spin his head toward it, his grip on the tool swinging as he would normally point his gun in reaction to a foreign sound. But as he swung toward the sound, the device hit the edge of the opening and began to fall. His lightning reflexes quickly recover the device, but in the process, he cut his hand on the sharp edge of the open metal panel. Like being cut with a freshly honed butcher knife – it was a clean but very deep cut and his hand was bleeding profusely onto the droid with large droplets landing on the floor.

The partial pulse was not enough to fully disable the droid, but Art had no idea it was only partially decommissioned, his concern was his DNA creating small puddles on the floor.

"DAMNIT," said Art as he looks down and sees blood pools on the floor – this was not a simple scratch. *That's gonna leave a mark*, thinks Art as he drags the droid to the nearest heap and throws it on the pile.

"Piece of shit fucking droid!" Damone opens the coveralls, pulls off his tee-shirt, tore off a strip to wrap and contain the cut – the remainder of the shirt he dropped to the floor to mop up the blood. As he departs, holding his arm to his chest, he deposits the blood-soaked partial shirt in the trash bin. He knows he's going to need a stitch or two. His bandages are going to affect his trigger finger and grip, but this didn't concern Art, he's ambidextrous anyway.

Perhaps, he thinks, *I will take a brief vacation when this job is done. Maybe one of the islands of Fiji or Bali – someplace with fewer people and no droids...*

THE SHOPPING TRIP

The Dallas recycling warehouse is a series of long metal buildings surrounded by wire fencing that is easy to break through if someone wanted in, just a simple chain link. Unfold two wires untwist a single wire from the bottom up and the fence is now like a filleted fish. A person can then just lay back the sides to open the separated sections and walk through with the little folding hand cart.

This method of opening of the fence takes more time than a simple wire cutting, but Beth is with him as lookout today and it's already getting dark. With so many buildings they would likely be able to salvage then reclose the laid open fence, to avoid detection and provide an opportunity for a possible return if this facility is particularly laden with droids. They have learned the pickup schedules for the crushed droids, so their shopping trips are usually planned to maximize their haul and avoid any hint of their having been there.

Once inside you see piles of droids – not so neatly stacked but rather unceremoniously dumped by the forklift full. There is plenty of dirt from the daily operation involving forklifts moving the haphazard heaps of droids to more manageable piles that will later be stripped of power modules and moved outside to the yard where they will be crushed in preparation for transport to metal recycling facilities. The recycling warehouse is not technically a recycling facility but pre-cycling storage and transfer station.

The droids have been decommissioned, their power supplies interrupted and rendered non-operational like the stopped heart of a human prepared for bypass surgery, except in the case of these droids, their vital functions are not being sustained awaiting the lifesaving power to be restored. Once they have been decommissioned, their body shells are dumped by the bucket loader into large crushers that yield easily stackable cubes. The cubes get shipped by big rig trucks to transport to rail centers where the loaded flatbeds are deposited onto rail transports destined for smelting locations that will repurpose the scrap metal.

Josh and Beth were busily removing components and circuit boards with a practiced efficiency of a surgical team. Their skills were efficient results from the many missions they had done. They were familiar with the recycling centers across Dallas and Fort Worth, Texas. As always, Beth's attention to their surroundings was her primary focus. Today, however, she sees something she hadn't ever seen before. In her peripheral vision, she noticed a faint glow – a blinking light, but not a bright light – just not a light she has seen before in any of their salvaging/shopping expeditions.

She notified Josh in a hushed voice, that she has found something needing his attention. Josh, replies with a whisper, "Be careful."

Suddenly she, in a not so hushed voice calls to Joshua. "Hey, there is something here! It's a DROID I think!" Joshua quickly stopped what he was doing because Beth rarely interrupted him when he was salvaging.

"Of course it's a droid – duh… Beth, what else would you think you would find in here?" His voice was still quiet but it was clear that he was annoyed at the interruption to his work.

"I THINK IT'S AN MSA DROID!!!," she exclaimed excitedly, "and it's still showing some activity."

What she had found was indeed an MSA model droid, one that was not fully decommissioned. The MSA's (medical services assistant androids) are rarer than an HA model (home assistant) or DS model (domestic service).

The most common was the DP models, designed for domestic pleasure. When they found the DPs, they didn't bother with them – they rarely had salvageable parts. Josh didn't know if this was because they were not built to the same standard, or just that they worked harder than other droids, but he'd only scraped out a couple DP's before determining that they weren't worth bothering with.

He stopped what he was doing to respond to her non-typical urgent and calling out to him. MSA blinks the eyes. *This droid is not fully decommissioned!* "HOLY DROID!" whispers Josh. Now rather than collecting parts and printed circuits, their mission is radically changed, they must liberate the entire droid, it is "alive" in human terms, yet, it is immobile. About the size of an average human female and weighing as much, it will not be as easy to move as their normal boxes of salvaged small parts.

"Beth!!!! You got the golden ticket! We are gonna have to get this droid out of here and I'm gonna need your help on this."

The decommission process involved high current, most often this current destroys many semi-conductor parts that Josh would love to have been able to salvage. Something went wrong during the decommissioning process with this droid. For Josh, this was like finding the Holy Grail. With a little effort, he might be able to have his functional droid!

Josh quickly dumped the contents from the cart and returned for the droid. If it could only walk, thinks Josh, but sadly that is not the case. The droid is partially decommissioned so he and Beth needed to manhandle the inert droid to get it onto the hand cart to move it.

As they partially lift and shove the droid onto the cart, Beth's hand slipped off the droid. *Maybe hydraulic fluid from the droid*, she pondered. It appeared to be a darkish color in the minimum security lighting of the warehouse.

No time to check that now as they needed to get this droid out of this building and to the car without being discovered. They had never taken a whole droid before. Considering that these droids were destined for the smelting process, Josh didn't think there was that much value in the metal of a single droid, and smelters didn't care about the components. This partially working droid would have been scooped and dumped into the metal crusher hopper with no notice of its operational status.

Getting the droid to the fence was easy with the hand cart, but the manual push and pull effort needed to get it through the fence and into the trunk proved to be the most challenging part of their day so far.

When they got the droid loaded into the trunk, Beth noticed the reason for the slipping inside the warehouse. She has blood on her hands.

Blood? Droids don't bleed, thinks Beth.

JOSHUA'S HOUSE

MSA121068 is trying to send a message with blinks of the eye modules. MSA blinks blinks blinks – *Oh these humans, so illogical, why do they not understand?*

As Beth peers into the eyes of MSA very closely she says –"Josh, I think it is Morse code. Look at the eyes, sometimes the blinks are long and sometimes short. Like maybe it's sending SOS!" MSA's eyes are blinking:

```
01010010  01000101  01000011  01001111
01001101  01001101  01001001  01010011
01010011  01001001  01001111  01001110
00100000  01000011  01001111  01000100
01000101  00100000  00110110  00110001
00110010  00110100  00111001  01001101
00110101  00110001  00110110  00110101
00111001  01000010  00100000  01001101
01010101  01010011  01010100  00100000
01010011  01000001  01010110  01000101
00100000  01001101  01000001  01001110
01001011  01001001  01001110  01000100
```

The blinks include a slow blink followed by three short blinks then two slow, etc. "Hmmm," says Beth, "well the code seems to be longer than S.O.S doesn't it?" Joshua comes for a closer look. "Let me get a good look," as he peers at the eye modules like an ophthalmologist looking into the macula at the interior of an eye. "No," says Joshua, "It's not Morse code, droids were never taught Morse code. That is too military – too antiquated to be used in a droid. Droids are programmed, Beth. No self-respecting civilian programmer would use Morse code. That's for emergency signals for ships or planes in distress or any dumb campers that get lost hiking on a mountain with no jacket or shovel."

"Well, could it be ASCII?" Beth is sort of proud of the fact she knows a bit of computer lingo now. "Could be," says Josh, "let's hope it is ASCII. ASCII was from the very early times of computers, but it stuck like glue, I must record the message so I can find the beginning and end of the message. Beth, you need to try to find out who was the owner of this droid while I work on the message."

Over the past couple of years, Joshua had managed to coach her in computer searching. Her increased knowledge about the droid and robot models and part numbers was instrumental in maximizing their income opportunities, as he called it. Josh grabbed his cell and puts it into video mode. "OK Mister MSA, start from the beginning please."

Beth gently says, "Josh, please refrain from calling it a Mister, this model of droid has no gender, and it wasn't built for pleasure!" Slightly irritated by the interruption Josh replied, "Beth, I can see that, no silicone cyber skin and no anatomical features. Get your mind out of the gutter. If I thought it was one of those, I'd have HER in the other room!" Beth throws her hands in the air as she walks over to the PC, "I don't know how you set me up like that!" And to herself, she thinks, *especially with a real human female just a few feet away*. To which Josh replies, "You set yourself up, Beth, now quiet, I'm trying to record the message so I can figure it out. Find the owner because when I get this video done, I'll need the PC to interpret the message."

"Sorry buddy," Josh says turning his attention to MSA, "please start again", as Josh began to take a video of the blinking message.

Beth searched several of her favorite droid media sites and finally finds the matching asset tag # MSA121068.

* * *

Utah

A thousand miles away in the desert of Utah, on a monitor in front of an NSA analyst, a message pops up.

```
SEARCH FOR MSA121068 DETECTED.
TRACKING IMPLEMENTED.
TRACKING IN PROGRESS........
```

The analyst quickly sent a text to his project leader.

* * *

Her next search led to the Doctor Ellison Hampton and the droid acquisition from MedServePro in Dallas, Texas. The acquisition was ordered to deliver the MSA to SAVIOR Labs, to the attention of Doctor Ellison D. Hampton. *That's an odd name for a laboratory*, thinks Beth.

Subsequent searches for Dr. Hampton got her hits on research papers about virology and epidemiology but all are more than 30 years old. Another attempt located a death notice in the Department of Vital Statistics with no family mentioned, nor a cause of death. "Oh he recently died, there is no listing for the cause of death – no obituary, this is odd – the simplest forensics exam can tell what type of toothpaste you used this morning so, why is there no cause of death? He wasn't that old," said Beth.

Josh didn't respond to her remark – he had a way of

shutting off the world when he was doing something that he deemed to be a higher priority. Beth thinks to herself: *Why would an MSA droid be in service in a lab named SAVIOR?* She should thank her lucky stars that she met Josh, there was no way she could have graduated college with her previous computer illiteracy.

After the observation about his obituary, she continued with her search and found the MedServePro website which had a pick box to download schematics. She clicked and waited as the download bar slid across the screen. Partway through the process, the page froze. She attempted everything she could think of to return to the schematic download button but discovered she couldn't even access the website now. She tried several different search options and nothing she did would gain her entrance into the MedServePro site now.

"Did you find the owner or supplier?" asks Josh.

"Hmmm', said Beth, 'I found that the model number and manufacture date at a manufacturing facility called MedServePro. I was downloading schematics but I guess I haven't learned the magic touch yet Josh."

Josh, "What do you mean Beth – you're a great little fact-finder lately – what magic touch don't you have?"

* * *

Utah

The NSA analyst, now constantly monitoring messages and relaying via secure text messages to the project lead, received the order to terminate the activity.

He entered a series of commands the monitor display shows:

```
CONTINUE TRACKING.
SEARCH VIOLATION SOURCE.
TERMINATE VIOLATION ACTIVITY.
SCHEMATIC DOWNLOAD - STOP.
```

```
DOWNLOAD VIOLATION STOP - EXECUTED.
VIOLATION IP ADDRESS - TRACKING......
```

* * *

Beth replied, "Well, I was downloading the schematics and somehow I got disconnected. I don't know if I got a complete set of documents, do you want me to try again?"

"Just put what you have on a scan disk, never mind, I'll do it, I'm going to need the computer in a minute or two." Relinquishing the computer to the wizard called Josh, she quietly says "Josh – You make me want to be a better web navigator." Josh replied, "Beth, you were computer challenged in college, but when you work with a genius long enough, something has to rub off."

He quickly loads the partial schematic file onto the SD then returns to his goal of converting the blink code he'd recorded. A short while later, "FINALLY!!' he happily yells, "Beth – I've got it – the message is binary!!!!." "Show me," said Beth. Josh played the video – slowing it down slightly then tapped the series of zeros and 1's into the converter program. Simultaneously the converter yields the message:

"RECOMMISSION CODE 61249M51659B
MUST SAVE MANKIND"

They were both were speechless, mouths open, staring in disbelief at what was in front of them. Not the recommission code number, but the "MUST SAVE MANKIND"!

DECOMMISSIONED

FBI DC CONFERENCE ROOM

Michael Carver (Director FBI) and his assistant Travis Loki are seated at a table with General Alan Rockwell, in one of the FBI SKIF locations. On the wall are securely linked monitors set to display the meeting attendees via encrypted satellite communication. The video conferencing software provides for each representative to be able to see the others present.

Carver: "Ladies and gentlemen, thank you for your presence for this very important meeting. I believe you all know each other, but I will ask you each, to introduce yourself for the record, your agency, and your title. Stephanie, please start by introducing yourself."

"Stephanie Wolff – Director NSA – Thank you all for being here." (video)

"Chuck Delphi – (DOD) Assistant to Director Roger Ackinsen who is not present here today."

"Travis Loki – Assistant to Director Michael Carver FBI"

"General Alan Rockwell – U.S. Army" (video)

"Emmett Rankin – Director CDC." (video)

"Joanna Moore – CEO RiverMoore Laboratories." (video)

"Michael Carver – Director FBI. Others invited but not in attendance: Roger Ackinsen, Director DOD, and Darla Avery, Director CIA. Those, not in attendance will be included in secured meeting notes and correspondence."

Michael Carver (FBI) continued by asking Emmett Rankin (CDC) to speak. Emmett Rankin, "Ladies and gentlemen, I will get directly to the point of this meeting. It is because the CDC has the utmost concern for national security as it relates to a possible epidemic of a deadly virus. What we have today is a situation potentially involving the health of the entire population of the United States of America. It is probably best if Miss Moore, CEO RiverMoore Laboratories of Dallas gets us started by sharing with us her knowledge of the virus. When she is finished we will address your questions."

Miss Moore on the video monitor begins to speak, "I believe that all present know about the JMV2030 bio-virus developed at RiverMoore Laboratories. The JMV2030 was designed and manufactured for international bio-warfare. It appears however that the JMV2030 bio-virus may have been disseminated within the United States population. RiverMoore has not discovered how the JMV2030 has infected U.S. civilians nor where it was released to the public from.

The virus was manufactured by RiverMoore, it was transported and stored at Bearlywoke, and the development of anti-virus effort was performed at SAVIOR Labs. So we have three possible locations where this accident could have happened. RiverMoore has completed a strenuous evaluation of its security protocol and determined that there was no possible breach at that location. It is not in my authority to execute similar investigations into the security measures employed at Bearlywoke Storage or SAVIOR Labs.

What we know, is that the virus is not sufficiently virulent to exist long outside a living host. As such, the virus is not designed to be an epidemic as with airborne flu viruses such as the bird flu, swine flu, SARS, or Covid-19.

An accidental infection could only happen if a very sick patient in extreme proximity were to contaminate others with a sneeze or wet cough. As previously stated, this virus is NOT a lingering airborne virus. And bear in mind gentlemen, that the mortality period from exposure to death is designed for and expected to be very short. In a controlled environment using lab animals, we are talking about less than eight hours.

An infected human would last longer – perhaps up to 24 hours nominally depending on the overall health of the individual, but lethal nonetheless. We currently only have computer modeling of the expected response in humans because we have not received any field testing data.

Remembering that this virus was developed to be used as a military bio-weapon, the design was intended to be fast and anonymous. Naturally, we ordered the development of an effective vaccine to protect our military assets, who would ultimately be at a minor chance of exposure in offshore military deployment areas.

This task of the creation of anti-virus has been in the testing phase in laboratory animals by an epidemiologist, Doctor Ellison Hampton, at SAVIOR Labs, Fort Worth Texas. Doctor Hampton informed us ninety days ago that the anti-virus treatment drug testing in lab animals had reached 97 percent effectiveness with computer models indicating similar numbers. Ten days ago his communication indicated that the drugs were ready for enemy combatant human testing on non-USA soil."

Joanna is thinking as she is speaking - *CIA, the US Army CENTCOM, and DOD have been informed and should be in the process of executing the field testing why is the CIA not represented here in this meeting? They should have reports of the effectiveness of the ongoing field testing.* "Unfortunately, we have been unable to contact Dr. Hampton after repeated attempts. Our last contact was six days (as she looks at her watch) and three hours ago. Doctor Hampton is a DOD asset and I believe there needs to be some investigation by the FBI and CIA to locate Dr. Hampton. I believe his disappearance falls under the category of national security. His laboratory has been funded in part by the NSA, DOD, FBI, and CDC. I would like to know why Doctor Hampton is not in attendance here as his input is vital to the content of this meeting."

Michael Carver (FBI): "Thank you, Miss Moore and I assure you that all necessary resources will be devoted to the location and debriefing of Dr. Hampton. You will be advised when the doctor's whereabouts are discovered. The remainder of this meeting will be at a higher level of security than your current credentials permit. So thank you again, I will be in touch." Her remote connection is terminated.

To put it plainly, Joanna was offended in a very big way. She is, after all, the CEO of RiverMoore Labs, the same RiverMoore Labs that houses the most lethal bacteria and viruses known around the world. The same laboratory that is responsible for the creation of this virus. *What could these government bigwigs be discussing that was beyond the prevue of the designer of the virus presently being discussed?* She is not simply a CEO, she is a scientist, but obviously, *certain civilians are not considered valuable in the world of the government!* She was furious and now sitting with nothing to do but deal with the unanswered questions in her mind about the attendance of certain integral players who should have been in that meeting.

FBI MEETING CONTINUED

Emmett Rankin of the CDC continues (after Moore has been disconnected):

"So what I have to say here is that medical tracking indicates that bio-virus JMV2030 may have been introduced to a minimum of 34 civilian victims, so far, all terminal, all in the general vicinity of SAVIOR Labs and/or Bearlywoke Storage.

The reason I say 'may have' is because the medical community has received no information about the existence or effects of JMV2030. Please bear in mind that this virus was developed for military use on non-American soil. In short, there was no 'need-to-know' within the U.S. civilian medical institutions.

This need-to-know status may be the reason the local medical professions are seeing a slight rise in afflictions related to the virus, as such, they have no point of reference or experience from which to conclude. The resulting manifestation of the virus affects the human body in a variety of organ attacks, so the lack of similarity in symptoms and cause of death is not recognizable to the uninformed civilian medical community.

Soon, I'm going to need the authorization to provide instructions on how to recognize what treatment protocol to employ. The CDC is getting reports and questions from the greater Dallas Fort Worth facilities asking for CDC to come in to evaluate what they are seeing. They aren't suggesting a virus, only that what they are seeing is abnormal.

CDC needs immediate access to SAVIOR Labs and Bearlywoke to get any existing stores of anti-virus for distribution to the currently affected areas, in addition to the formula for immediate manufacture of quantities larger than anticipated for military application."

Carver interrupted Doctor Rankin at this point. "Mr. Rankin, this is not going to happen. We understand there are many affected but that they are target area-specific and we cannot qualify the need for a nationwide alert to be unleashed at this time. The last thing we need is a national panic – it is my understanding that the current dissemination is a very limited area out in Texas. Of course, if you feel compelled to be proactive, I would strongly suggest that you impose extreme security as you develop any planned public release of information. Perhaps you should limit your interaction to the target area medical community to prevent initiating a public hysteria."

Mr. Rankin chose his battle by diverting to DOD and asking Mr. Delphi, "Mr. Delphi, would it be asking too much to inquire how much packaged anti-virus Bearlywoke has in storage and how fast more can be prepared?"

Mr. Delphi responds, "I regret that I don't have access to that information at this moment in time."

Rankin continues to address the remaining group: "When this meeting is concluded I must have approval for a team to develop and launch material instructions to advise hospitals to employ a safety protocol, as they wait to receive anti-virus serum. They need to be informed that antibiotics are useless against the virus. And I need to be able to tell them with confidence that there is sufficient anti-virus ready to be delivered.

I see Mr. Ackinsen is not present, though I assume he has been informed of the missing Dr. Hampton. Mr. Delphi, I hope that Mr. Ackinsen has something very important happening that he was unable to attend here today. Are you in the position of Acting Director here?"

Delphi, "Yes, I am, and I will be giving Mr. Ackinsen a full accounting of the meeting immediately upon his return to DOD. I will of course get you a report today of anti-virus inventory at Bearlywoke. Regrettably, I am not privileged to know how much if any anti-virus is housed at SAVIOR Labs they are the research entity – not manufacturing. But I can get back to you with what is stored in Bearlywoke. As to the authorization to release information regarding safety protocol to medical administrative directors, of course, you have approval for this Mr. Rankin."

Rankin continued, "CDC needs to access Doctor Hampton to quarantine both he and SAVIOR Labs to discover if the bio-virus was released from that facility. We already have field agents on their way to Bearlywoke with orders to possibly quarantine and assess its security. RiverMoore has already been cleared. Are there any questions?"

The participants were silent

Mr. Michael Carver FBI, "Thank you, Emmett, for addressing the CDC position, I'm sure you need to get to those quarantines. As soon as we find Hampton, we will contact both you and Miss Moore immediately."

Rankin is dismissed – slightly suspicious over the abrupt dismissal and conference disconnection – *there is something amiss here and I am not a part of it.* He's been around the government long enough to have pretty thick skin. *They don't consider CDC to be part of the government, just a necessary evil, but Joanna was furious. I'm thinking I might need to touch base with her this evening. No questions at all about the number of casualties – their locations or duration of the time from discovery to mortality. These people should have plenty of questions*, thinks Rankin. *I have plenty of questions!*

Only members of the highest security level remain now as Carver gets to the serious business at hand. Carver continues, "General Rockwell, Dr. Hampton is missing –all sitting here understand the reason for his absence is his demise, please enlighten us on the pertinent details."

General Allan Rockwell, "Sir, I would like to state for the record that the US Army was not involved in the removal of the Doctor nor advised of the reason for the action. The Army is not involved in the assassinations of citizens. But that being said, it is my understanding that a private contractor was employed for the task plus an additional order for the decommissioning and disposal of the MSA. There was, apparently, a SNAFU and the droid is missing.

The contractor tasked with the removal and decommissioning of the MSA had an accident at the recycle center which dictated his temporary absence for medical treatment. When he returned, the droid was gone."

Carver, "Well shitfire! What do you mean, Hampton's MSA is missing? That damn droid has the contents of all Hampton's research, that droid knows how all there is to know about the virus. Droids don't just go missing – especially one that is decommissioned – so where the hell is it?"

Rockwell to Carver, "Well my reports, Sir, indicate that the MSA was transported to the recycle location as I previously stated. But, the recycle location now reports that their records show the incoming MSA121068 but no recycle performed AND MSA121068 is not found on the premises. At this time, Sir, I have assets converging on the recycle location to find the BOT."

Carver's face is the color of a freshly boiled lobster, "IT

IS NOT A BOT YOU DUMBASS – IT IS AN MSA DROID and it quite possibly contains the formula to the anti-virus for an agent that can selectively destroy mankind! And you are telling me that you have no idea where it is? What kind of half-ass story are you telling me that a droid can simply be....."

Rockwell (now also angered at the "dumbass" comment) interrupted: "SIR, The Army HAS NOT received any orders regarding the bug, and though we are privileged to know of its existence, we HAVE NOT received any vaccines OR bio-med agents. NOR have we received any communications regarding when or how we are to begin offshore human testing. We expect YOU are going to need the assistance of the National Guard if this bug isn't controlled......so it might serve you well to temper your remarks accordingly, SIR."

Carver, calmly, "At this point, I need you to follow up on the missing droid. The Texas Governor will contact you immediately if it becomes necessary to deploy the National Guard. General Rockwell, the Army is best armed with plausible deniability; if you have nothing further to contribute you are excused."

And with that – the Army has been excused.

Carver, "Is Rankin going to find anything when he goes snooping around SAVIOR Labs?"

Delphi to Carver, "No, sir – The doctor was moved to the medical examiner's cold storage. The droid is missing, and SAVIOR Labs only holds a small amount of the raw virus and anti-virus in addition to the randomized stuff. There's nothing there for Rankin to get his panties in a twist over."

Stephanie Wolff from NSA interrupted Carver, "Gentlemen, Gentlemen - Excuse me gentlemen, but reports coming into my office show that there have been inquiries into the cause of Hampton's death, we are in the process of tracking down the source of the inquiries.

Stephanie received a text. "Well, that is interesting." Almost in unison – Carver and Delphi ask, "What's interesting?" Stephanie, "Someone has hacked into the MedServePro droid schematic database! The search was for an MSA model schematic. And it looks like they are also investigating Dr. Hampton and his cause of death." She now sends a text to the analyst to continue tracking the source and shut down the search activity.

Carver (FBI), "We must find that MSA before someone recommissions it – and I'd like to know Hampton's published cause of death? Someone needs to find out who the hell is snooping into the doctor– it could be the person who has the droid! There's gonna be some ass-kicking going on if we don't clean this up and FAST."

Stephanie responds, "On it, director, I already have a reliable analyst on the task."

"Loki," says Carver, "get me a secure line to DOD Ackinsen and conference in Darla Avery at CIA, I'm not gonna bend over on this alone!!!"

Loki (who is Carver's assistant) quietly reminded Carver, "Sir, Mr. Ackinsen is currently unavailable and the CIA is only involved in international issues."

Carver's response is speedier than a patriot missile, "I know that, but at this point, we don't know who has the MSA – it could be in the hands of foreign agents. So yes by God, it could very well be an international issue. DO it! DO it YESTERDAY! Nobody is getting any rest until we locate and contain whoever has the MSA. We all have work to do – meeting dismissed."

GENERAL ROCKWELL

After having been dismissed from the call, Rockwell is still stewing. *I am used to taking orders and I've been cussed out more times than I can count in my 30-year career in the Army. But I have three stars in front of General and I will continue to be a three-star General long after this little dipshit Carver is replaced by the next president in less than one year.*

After taking a deep breath, he is ready to speak with his aide, Staff Sargent James Wright. "So where are we with chasing down the tin can droid, Wright?"

Wright, "Sir, we got nothing. We went to the warehouse – the droid came in, but the guy who runs the place says the agent that brought it, took it to do the decommission himself. The yard guy said he never saw any follow-up paperwork. He's kinda pissed because we won't let him crush and clear his yard or send off to scrap recycle until we've verified every asset number. But we told him to get over it, if he moves a single droid, we are gonna be on him like stink on shit for impeding a military operation. So far we have checked asset numbers on 1250 droids and that the MSA just isn't there.

Additionally, we found a breach in the perimeter and

possible vehicle tracks. It looks like the droid was removed, but by whom we have no clue. Blood was found in the recycling center, not sufficient quantities to suggest a homicide. This supports the claim of an accident, but DNA search has come up negative for a name, so far."

Rockwell, "Yes, Wright, I already had that recycle incident information, before my meeting. Is there anything else?"

Wright, "Only that the agent is now also missing."

Rockwell, "SHIT!!! Wright – is that information written down anyplace?"

Wright, "No sir, do you want me to…."

Rockwell, "NO!! The fricking FBI can't keep track of their own hired guns, we are not gonna do it for them. Neither of us heard that part about the missing agent – got it?"

"Got what agent, sir? Never heard about any agent sir," said the loyal Staff Sergeant Wright.

DELPHI - DOD

Gracie Valentine: "Joanna Moore on the line Mr. Delphi, would you like me to take a message?"

Delphi, "Christ on a Cracker!!! I'd love you to take a message but that woman is a pit-bull – that bitch would track me down to the locked stall of the men's room! Get me a scotch – neat – better yet bring me the bottle. Thanks, Gracie."

This is gonna be a conversation that he is not going to enjoy. So he turned on his 'sugar voice' reserved for pandering to females he considered to be mentally beneath a piss ant.

Delphi picked up the phone, "Heyyyyyy there Joanna, great reporting on the virus situation earlier. Sorry, you had to disconnect so early after your presentation. It's pretty boring being in a meeting without your pretty face. I've got Carver's peeps looking for your missing Doctor."

Delphi is under the misimpression that he is a charmer of women. He mistakenly believes he can take her off guard with his flirtatious repartee, but Joanna is smarter than the above-average bull-shitter.

Joanna, "Spare me, Delphi – I'm not in the mood for a song and dance!"

Delphi mumbled under his breath, "Pitbull"

Joanna, "Excuse me – did you say something?"

Delphi, "No ma'am, just moved the phone."

Joanna continues now ticking off her questions by number,

"Number 1, why did Carver boot me?

Number 2, was it Bearlywoke or SAVIOR Labs that let the virus out?

Number 3, where the hell is Doctor Hampton.

Number 4, when was the last transfer between SAVIOR Labs and Bearlywoke.

Number 5, how many dead civilians are there?"

Delphi is shaking his head while Joanna rolled off the questions, but these rapid-fire questions are very good news to him, it means she doesn't know that the Doctor is dead OR that the MSA is missing. She isn't aware of the individual or individuals seeking information on the MSA and the doctor. BUT she does seem to know about dead civilians. These facts are bonuses for Delphi because it's a chance to blow her off and close the lines of communication with her until, *hmmmmm*, thinks Delphi, *until it becomes necessary to decommission her.*

Delphi, "Geez Joanna, you are asking a lot, I've only been back from the meeting for about 15 minutes. I haven't even written a report for Ackinsen yet." Delphi's bottle arrived and he blew a kiss to Gracie before continuing. "I can probably get some sanitized answers to your questions but it's going to take some time. Ackinsen isn't going to let me share certain levels of secure information. Christ, I expect some of your requests are above MY security clearance. But I promise I'll get you what I can, 'cause you know I've always had a crush on you."

Joanna, "UP YOURS Delphi!" as she hung up on him.

Delphi just pours himself a triple, gonna need courage for the next call. "Gracie sweetheart, can you get Ackinsen on the secure line for me? And messages only from Miss Moore until further notice – that bitch really is a boner-killer. You think we can fix that problem, Sugar?"

"Ten-Four Chuck,"…says Gracie with a wink and a suggestive smile. They both know it is only a question of time before she will be spreading her legs for him again. They know that's the only way to move up in this place and for Gracie Valentine, nothing else has worked so far.

Carver is starting to slip, thinks Chuck, *he's making mistakes that put us at risk, having that dumbass General in the meeting, we can't have the Army sticking their noses in and sniffing around this Clearcut Project. I'm going to have to discuss this with Ackinsen and he might not like where this is going either.*

DECOMMISSIONED

DELPHI ON THE PHONE TO ACKINSEN

"Mr. Ackinsen, I just got reamed by Joanna Moore. She's got her nose out of joint because Carver dismissed her from the meeting rather than Emmett. I think she believes that because she runs a petri dish that she's in the same league with CDC. But the reason I called is not that her feelings are hurt. She asked…. No demanded specific questions: Where is Hampton? How many dead civilians so far? So riddle me this – does she need to be contained? Do you need me to call Travis Loki to get the ball rolling on the decommissioning of the petri dish? He knows how to get in touch with contractors."

Ackinsen, "Thanks Chuck, I think this is above his pay grade – I'll have to call Carver myself, he will have to be the one to make the call, sanitizing a CEO is going to take a level of finesse that only the FBI can manage. For the time being, try to keep Miss Moore calm, send her some flowers or something. Hell, fly to Dallas and take her to dinner – you know how to calm a woman. We don't need a Sherlock Holmes sniffing around."

Delphi continues, "Oh and another question I have for you, does the Army know about Clearcut? General

Rockwell was in the meeting and he seemed to be out of the loop. He knows Hampton was dispatched, but not why, and he's wondering why the Army hasn't gotten instructions for the testing start time and use of the bio-weapon. I think Carver is losing it – bringing someone into the meeting who is out of the loop. I mean, Rankin and Moore were there but they got dismissed before anything secret was discussed. I'm wondering if Carver is slipping if you get my drift. It was good that he had the sense to dismiss Rankin and Moore – no damage done there, but I don't know what to make of what happened about Rockwell. He sort of dismissed him suggesting the reason was plausible deniability. That is a bell ringer to a three-star general. I wish he hadn't done that. You tell three-stars they are out and suggest deniability - it is a dinner bell for brass. The only thing they can do at that point is to bring in the bloodhounds. I think it's in their DNA – is there such a thing as 'suspicion DNA'? Because I have to say, it doesn't take much to get the military with their noses sniffing the air."

Ackinsen, "The Army is not privy to the details of Clearcut; the generals' involvement is primarily regarding the use of the bio-weapon. This is going to go public, so it was important to involve him at the beginning of the upcoming crisis, which will certainly involve the National Guard. I may need to see Carver in person to find out if he had a reason for the 'plausible deniability' statement, but it seems like it might have been meant to set the general at ease knowing that fingers won't be pointed at him."

Delphi, "Yes it will go public, but I'm just a little uncomfortable with Rockwell getting blindsided when it could have been avoided. I don't know why he was present at this point. We can't afford any leaks."

Ackinsen, "Well I guess it was on me that Rockwell was there – because he will need to be on top of the Guard when the rioting starts. Oh, how quick can you get me a transcript of the meeting? You know I don't have a poker face so my presence there would have been dangerous. This shit hitting the fan is giving me heartburn."

Chuck is thinking, *Sherlock Moore is looking for inventory transfer between RiverMoore, Bearlywoke, and SAVIOR Labs, it might be a good idea to doctor some records or perhaps make them disappear, in the unlikely event Sherlock gets too close to Clearcut. Well, she is just a petri dish — our records will show that the amount of randomized virus is equal to the bulk of what was NOT used by the doctor anyway — so why bother?*

DECOMMISSIONED

JOANNA MOORE

Joanna is very concerned about how the virus got released to the public and equally about how to find the good Doctor who has the antivirus and vaccination formulae that need to be manufactured and distributed. Joanna is thinking to herself: *RiverMoore Laboratories has a lot invested in the creation of this virus, now THEY (being the government) want to put the genie back in the bottle.*

She is aware of the growing numbers of medically suspicious deaths. The medical field is not aware of the virus, but SHE knows it was RiverMoore that developed the virus! *They didn't even blink when I told them that Dr. Hampton had developed the anti-virus and randomized formulae and that he now is missing* - (click went her brain). *They didn't inquire how many deaths have happened* (click) (click), *where the deaths occurred (click), or what actions RiverMoore had taken thus far to discover how the virus is loose* (click). (click) (click) (click) – Joanna is mentally counting the dead ends – *Something is amiss here.* She has seen to thorough testing of the RiverMoore facility to find if the release might have been a RiverMoore accident – that RiverMoore could be culpable. *But they didn't ask any questions about that either* - (click) (click).

She has already poured over surveillance records, computer records of employee logs in and out, facility cyber activity. There had been nothing, not a shred of evidence pointing to a possibility of a breach at RiverMoore. Before she attended the meeting, every one of her employees from all shifts including security staff, had been contacted to be tested for fever or other cold type symptoms. Everyone was clean.

Everything possibly related to a compromise has been collected to bless her desk with piles of reports which will be her focus rather than sleep tonight. She had even shared this employee testing information with Rankin before the meeting, stating that RiverMoore was clean. Not a single question from the members present in that meeting about what she had done to verify that RiverMoore was not culpable for the release. If SHE had been heading up that meeting, there would have been at least an hour devoted to inquiries into this and other questions of anyone who had the slightest involvement with the handling or transport of the virus. *Why did no one inquire what my efforts were to determine if RiverMoore was a possible source of the compromise?* (click)...

Joanna's mind is logically listing the items that simply don't add up to an accident. Finally, she decided that unanswered questions or lists were not going to prevent the loss of American lives! She must coordinate her actions with Rankin at CDC. First thing in the morning, she must prepare a manifest detailing exactly how much JMV2030 left RiverMoore to Bearlywoke DOD storage facility. She needed to know when and how much was transferred to SAVIOR in addition to the burning question, whether or not Bearlywoke had anyone presently ill or dead from mishandling or transfer of the virus.

She had no power to get information about Bearlywoke or SAVIOR Labs employee health issues, but the CDC would be able to access records and require testing of all employees in both facilities.

RiverMoore had been culturing and transferring JMV2030 since 6/2028. Why now is it showing itself in the U.S.A.? To her knowledge, it had never been used in combat. According to her records, Hampton had only recently cleared the anti-virus and approved the JMV2030R for non-USA soil, enemy combatant testing. *Dr. Hampton has just recently declared the 97percent positive response of the anti-virus at SAVIOR Labs* (click) (click) *– So yes – it should at least have been targeted to begin field testing in another country right now.* (click) *So why didn't the brass sitting there in the meeting discuss live field testing* (click)?

She turned the television on – just for a minute – to try to clear her head of that swimming feeling resulting from the piles of files and questions with no answers. *I need a break*, thinks Joanna. Every channel is reporting about the suspicious death of a renowned epidemiologist, Dr. Ellison Hampton. Reporters do not yet know the exact time or cause of death but at this time, foul play has not been ruled out, according to inside information. (click) (click) goes Joanna's brain, *We got trouble with a capital T! Doctor Hampton dead?* Nobody had called her to advise her of this.

I'm going to have to reach out to my contact at Bearlywoke. That is where the JMV2030 went, some of it for storage and to provide fast delivery for Dr. Hampton's testing and research. I need to find out when the last deliveries were made in addition to the shipping orders and location manifests to track volumes of the virus between Bearlywoke and SAVIOR Labs.

Joanna has poured through everything employee related for the 2nd time. She must also reiterate to Rankin that the medical community does not yet know about the virus or that Hampton had developed a 97 percent effective anti-virus. She had no idea how long ago the randomized virus had been complete, but it didn't seem like he would have ordered human testing until the anti-virus serum was thoroughly tested.

The anti-virus that must now be dispensed across the USA most expediently and it needs to start right here in Texas. At the top of her list of 'I want', she wanted to know if Rankin had been advised of Hampton's death.

She thought, *What time is it in Atlanta GA?* She knew she must call Rankin to share the information she has collated regarding the number of local deaths that she believes to be related to the virus. *Oh,* as she looked at her watch, *too late to call Georgia or D.C. Well, that will be the first item on the morning agenda.*

She needed to know the name of the Medical Examiner who processed the Doctor, because whoever that was would have no way of knowing about JMV2030 but surely have knowledge if the cause of his death was natural causes, or unusual or catastrophic system breakdown.

NORTH TEXAS MEDICAL EXAMINER

Since Joanna is a local Texan, she had already left a message with the Department of Public Safety to set up a meeting with Barbara Kaye Foster, who is the current Medical Examiner for Northern Texas. Barbara was pretty busy, but since Joanna's message was about CDC, she decided she'd better respond quickly and she had agreed to a meeting at the Department of Public Safety building as soon as possible.

At the Dallas Safety building, Joanna Moore met with Barbara who is a 60-something-year-old retired nurse now Medical Examiner. Barbara expressed her regrets that she doesn't have much time, so she would appreciate it if Joanna would get directly to the point of the visit.

Joanna, "Miss Foster, I appreciate your making yourself available on such short notice. My need to contact you is related to a very sensitive issue. I am involved in the investigation of possible viral concerns and the death of Doctor Elliott Hampton. Our records show you as the examiner. The CDC and I need to know what your diagnosed cause of death was. The vital statistics listed no cause of death and he was intimately involved with the processing of an extremely dangerous virus. For this reason, the CDC felt it was best to investigate the findings in the autopsy. Miss Foster, did you find anything unusual in the processing of the Doctor Hampton?"

Barbara Foster, "Well, I'll tell you what I know if you tell me what you know 'cause this is, ohhhhhhhhhhh child, so bad. His internal organs, well they just was like a total train wreck - broke down like someone opened up a whole BAG of bacteria that went to work on all manner of his organs. They was all sorts of things wrong with this boy, he got signs of serious colon problems, pneumonia, lung infection, and heart issues that was the most likely cause of death.

I got orders from some high-n- mighty, sweet-talkin bully from DOD tellin' ME that there 'will be no cause of death' and the body is gonna be collected as soon as I releases it, but I'm not to let nuthin' and nobody near it…! Now did you just say something about a virus bein' accidentally released???"

Joanna, "I said there is a possibility of a virus. Because there was no cause of death, we were interested in more specifics." Joanna did not like what sounded suspiciously like Delphi… telling the M.E. to falsify a cause of death and hide the body. "Do you have photos?"

Barbara, "HELLLL YEAH I GOT PHOTOS you think I'm stupid just 'cause I'm from a different country???"

Joanna, "Of course I assumed you had taken photos which would naturally be part of your job. What I meant to say was, may I see the photos?"

Barbara, "Oh ok, I worked hard to get where I am. This job is sorta my little kingdom so I get a lil bit thin-skinned when some gov'ment dick starts telling me my business. I spent mosta my adult life, people tellin me that I shouldn't expect for things to happen easy for me like might be for other persons. So when that joker in a suit, starts telling me what I need to put in a report and to hide the body until they can collect it up, well that dog just don't hunt..." Then she pulls an envelope from a file – it is filled with photos.

Joanna looks at them and quietly asked if there are any other bodies Miss Foster had recently examined that might have had similar oddities. "I showed you mine, you show me yours......" said Barbara.

Joanna opened her bag and withdrew an envelope with photos – lab animals opened up – barely discernable tissue where organs used to be. "I have no photos of any human autopsies because to this point, the virus was only used in laboratory animals. Barbara, I need copies of your photos, I don't have a warrant, but it is very important for me not to have to go that route because the time it would take, not to mention the risk of information being disseminated that is the better-left secret at this time. Was there anything else about the doctor that you can tell me?"

Barbara, "Lawwwd help me! The doctor and every other one of these I've examined got an injection. The others on the arm like a childhood vaccination, but this doctor – his was on his neck and they was two marks there and evidence of chloral hydrate in his blood. That bein' a Mickey Finn, Miss Moore.... Good night Mr. Doctor man 'fore the other injection. Do you know what a mickey....."

Joanna, "Yes Miss Foster, I am aware, thank you."

Barbara made copies of the photos and pulls out a stack of other files all full of reports and similar photos. Barbara, "Miss Moore, I got a stack of autopsy orders that's longer than your arm – I don't think your virus is a slow mover. From what I could figure, the mortality rate is only a few hours. The skin on most of these cadavers didn't even have rigor mortise yet on the ones I got called to test right away. That tells me that whatever is killing them breaks down organs fast – faster than normal – so normal rig doesn't apply when trying to figure out the time of death. Now I'm processing so many, I can't even dream of setting the times of death."

Joanna, "Were you able to approximate the time of death for Dr. Hampton?"

Barbara, "He has some minor rig starting so I guessed less than six hours. But the security guy, who called it in, said he didn't have a log file when he'd last seen the doctor. AND the security guy said for some reason – the security camera wasn't working so there's no video or timestamp info. It's not part of my job to investigate that kind of stuff, so I just didn't pay attention to it, but that security stuff is in the file.

This seems to have happened so fast that I don't think nobody but Jesus could know what time a person died from this 'whatever it is.' Now, Miss Moore – this is starting to smell to me – I'm too busy and I ain't been playing detective. So I think you need to start telling me what YOU know."

Joanna, "Miss Foster, what would you assess the cause of the doctor's death to be?"

Barbara, "Well, there was a lot of damage, but the primary seemed to be endocarditis – his heart was destroyed from the inside out. There were other organs in different stages of failure or decomposition, but the heart was the thing that killed him."

Joanna, "What about the others you've processed, endocarditis also?"

Barbara, "No ma'am – was a mixed bag of problems, some meningitis, encephalitis, hearts, but the rapid breakdown of, in all cases, involving multiple organs has been the common factor if you want my opinion but the variety of breakdowns wasn't consistent, there was nothing that pointed to a virus. There was nothing in the bloodwork to indicate a virus or infection – 'cept the Mickey Finn in the doctor – that was different."

Joanna put the files in her bag and told Barbara that she needs to be extremely careful, perhaps take a little vacation despite the volume of requests for autopsies that will be piling up.

Joanna, "Miss Foster, you have information that is extremely dangerous to the world but also for your safety."

Barbara, "I am careful in my lab, I'm not gonna pick up some bug…"

Joanna, "Barbara, I'm talking about your life, not your health. The government agencies who know about this bug will not let anyone put their operation at risk. Was the government dick named Chuck Delphi?"

Barbara, "Delphi – yeah, that was the name – never heard Chuck – Mistah Delphi…You sayin' that some secret agent is gonna try to get to me????? I bygod own a gun and knows hows to use it!"

Joanna, "I am just saying that you need to protect yourself from the enemy that you don't know, that if I were in your position, I would take my family and go on a very long and secret vacation. Your life is more important than a job. Here is my card – my phone number is on the back – call me once you get away from Dallas but please call from a payphone to let me know you are safe. And one last thing, do you think can switch tags or something, some way to keep the doctor's body from being collected? I have a feeling that Mickey Finn and the location of the injections could be proof that a murder was committed."

Barbara, "I can do that before I collect up my family, I will let you know the Doctor's new name."

Joanna, "Thank you, Miss Foster – please be safe."

Twenty –four hours later Joanna received a text message from a private caller on her cell phone.

"Come on in the water's fine – bring your friend J Doe IV"

Thank goodness, thinks Joanna, *Barbara will be safe there and now I know where to find the doctor.*

She immediately placed a call to a mortician she knows and asked to have J Doe #4 picked up from the Dallas morgue and put in isolated cold storage until she can make arrangements for a 2nd Medical examiner's opinion on the cause of death. The Dallas mortician tells her that he's pretty full right now – but he can transport to a different location over in Houston. He knows Houston isn't as busy as Dallas / Fort Worth right now. This suited Joanna just fine – she hadn't even considered that the locals would be overwhelmed. She tells him it is important that this transport is confidential with no paper trail.

EMMETT RANKIN - CDC

Rankin is pouring over the medical data that was collected during his meeting today. The 34 victim death toll he left this afternoon has now reached 46. That's 12 in less than six hours. Death by JMV2030 is not neat or slow. Rankin hasn't seen a victim yet, but Joanna had given a brief description of the destructive path of JMS2030.

It was engineered to kill fast – the catastrophic breakdown of internal organs by a variety of causes making it difficult if not impossible to isolate. There was no time for foreign agencies to effectively create an anti-virus or vaccine because the virus required living tissue to sustain itself – it killed itself in the process of destroying the host. The virus was designed to be airborne according to Miss Moore but only effective in close quarters, the virus couldn't live long without a human host which it quickly dispatched after its initial delay.

The victims had, according to the reports, no preliminary symptoms other than some initial minor cold or flu type of symptoms. The thing that made no sense to Rankin was the fact that there was no commonality of victims. A family member dies and nobody else in the family exhibits the slightest indication of symptoms. If the medical facilities had reported unhealthy people were more easily targeted by the virus, this would make sense to him. But the reports in front of him weren't showing anything that linked the deaths to exposure, genetics, or other systemic weaknesses such as immune deficiency disorders like Lupus, or HIV. Joanna had mentioned in the meeting about the remote possibility of the virus infecting by proximity to the sick.

From what he is reading – there has not been a single incidence of medical staff, caring for these sick and dying people becoming sick. There seemed to be no contracting the virus by exposure, although when the deaths began to occur, there were no quarantines invoked or special protective protocols in place. His desk was covered with charts and graphs, yet Rankin simply could not put a path between the victims and he was unable to connect the dots. There was no apparent commonality in the deaths.

He knew he would be reading incoming reports throughout the night and must try to ascertain a pattern. Joanna is thorough and she assessed her facility almost immediately after the first confirmed death which she had immediately reported to Rankin.

He must also start a plan to alert the U.S. population of the existence of a possible coming epidemic if steps weren't taken to vaccinate the public. There needed to be a coordinated effort, including a media blitz, to get people to medical facilities to receive the anti-virus vaccine. By the time the sun was coming up in DC, Rankin knew the first step in his plan needed to be the setup of a temporary field office in Fort Worth, Texas. He had to be close to the initial target area.

YĪSHĒNG AND RANKIN

When Emmett Rankin checked his messages, he found that Dr. Yīshēng Sǐwáng from Bearlywoke had left a message asking for an immediate return call regarding JMV2030.

When Rankin called him back, Dr. Yīshēng explained to Rankin that Bearlywoke had been preparing the virus for military distribution and since it had gotten released publicly (reasons presently unknown), that Center for Disease Control would be the most effective entity to mount the campaign to get the citizens to their medical facilities to receive the anti-virus vaccine. Yīshēng indicated his belief that the message would be better received from a CDC campaign than some non-governmental agency. He also reminds Rankin that a virus is a disease, regardless of where it began, and its existence needs to be communicated to the public, but the communication must be sugar-coated to avoid a nationwide panic.

Emmett resented the implication that the CDC needed to be advised on the need to communicate, but he held his temper.

Dr. Yīshēng, "Thank you Mr. Rankin for returning my call. I realize our time difference is a burden to communications. Considering that we have a crisis before us, I thought it best to make sure to initiate a dialog to ensure that our information is shared between our respective offices."

Rankin, "Dr. Yīshēng, of course, we must keep in close contact until we can squelch this virus problem. Perhaps you could help me by telling me the logistics of Bearlywoke Storage."

Dr. Yīshēng, "Bearlywoke is a manufacturing and storage location here in Highland Park, Texas. Our process is to receive and store the active virus JMV2030 from RiverMoore Laboratories (Dallas, Texas). The reason for our storage operation is to keep sufficient quantities of the virus to meet the needs of Doctor Ellison Hampton of SAVIOR Labs which is a very small operation. The Bearlywoke campus is in closer proximity to SAVIOR Labs and it is an extremely secure campus intended to protect the virus and serve as a manufacturing and distribution center once Dr. Hampton and his staff completed their research and development.

This virus was created to be used by the military as a biological weapon for use on foreign soil. Dr. Hampton had been responsible for the creation and testing of the corresponding anti-virus. The plan was for the weapon and its companion anti-virus to be packaged for the military, once the testing was completed and determined successful.

It is important to understand that DOD will be providing all necessary support to facilitate the media coverage necessary to tamp down a possibly riotous response. It is equally important, Mr. Rankin, to prevent the American public from becoming aware of the true purpose of the virus from which they currently need protection."

Dr. Yīshēng's suggestion to mount an aggressive campaign of public awareness based on a LIE conflicted with Carver's recommendation. The fact that the true reason for a viral epidemic was based on a false narrative infuriated Rankin. His next question was controlled despite his fury."

Rankin, "Thank you Dr. Yīshēng, this is information that has been provided to me by my staff. But I have a few questions that you might be able to respond to. We are aware that there have been many deaths possibly attributed to this virus, but my sources indicate these deaths are local. Do you have information indicating that there have been infections outside this immediate area? This knowledge is critical to my immediate task for the creation of local versus national media notifications."

Dr. Yīshēng, "Well at this moment, my sources indicate that the apparent viral target area is limited to the Fort Worth area, but I would temper that statement based on the aggressive behavior of the virus. I would not assume that targeting this limited location is going to be the end of the problem. If it were my task to prepare media material for medical and public conveyance, I would probably lean toward being proactive. Mr. Rankin, you have the ultimate decision when it comes to communicating important information to the medical and general public in matters of public health. I just felt that I needed to make you aware of my willingness to assist, as you respond to this crisis."

Rankin, "Doctor, in a recent meeting, it was suggested to me that 'because there is a limited target area, it was wise to 'tone communications down'. My position leans toward preparedness for a possible worst-case scenario. I am going to be setting up a temporary field office in Dallas to pursue more information preparatory to a possible media blanket project. It would be a great service to me if you would provide some statistics, such as inventory quantities of the anti-virus as well as how fast inventories might be increased.

I realize that the military need for the anti-virus would be smaller than that of the bio-weapon, but since the virus has been disseminated in the United States, I suspect we will need more anti-virus serum for immediate domestic needs.

I would appreciate the ability to meet with you later this week once I get moved to the satellite location. Perhaps we can discuss these needs by then. I hope that I will have better a perspective about the numbers of afflicted by then."

Dr. Yīshēng, "We will be pleased to show you Bearlywoke at your convenience and provide as much information as we are able. I am at your service Mr. Rankin."

Rankin, "Doctor, one more question if I may: do you believe the dissemination of JMV2030 was from SAVIOR?"

Dr. Yīshēng, "Mr. Rankin, I have full-time investigations ongoing, to eliminate Bearlywoke as the possible origin. As to the possibility of the virus being released from SAVIOR Labs, I could not speculate. Our relationship with that laboratory has been purely delivery of the raw virus for the research done at that facility until such time that the testing is completed. If I were in the position of CDC, I believe that I would have all employees of SAVIOR Labs quarantined and tested."

Rankin, "Doctor, do you know as to the level of completion of Dr. Hampton's testing? Was the virus being tested by the military? I'd like to know this, to consider if the release of the virus was perhaps an accident by the military?"

Dr. Yīshēng, "Mr. Rankin, it is my understanding that the virus was still not ready for human testing."

Rankin already knew the answer to his question. Joanna had said in the meeting that Dr. Hampton had reported that it was 97 percent and deemed it ready for field testing – just before he disappeared. Clearly, there was a question of veracity when it came to Dr. Yīshēng. Rankin now knows that any future information from Dr. Yīshēng must be considered as possibly 'lacking in candor'.

DECOMMISSIONED

MOORE AND RANKIN
COLLABORATION

Both Rankin and Joanna had been up all night trying to connect the dots of the stacks of reports and files of data. Emmett had sent a message, rather than call in the wee hours, to let Joanna know he would be arriving at Dallas by 10 AM where he would be setting up his temporary field office at the Marriott. His message requested that Joanna join him at her earliest convenience.

He flew by private jet so his workflow wasn't interrupted by standing in lines at an airport or neighboring passengers trying to make conversation. When he checked in at the hotel, he ordered a breakfast platter with Danish and fruit as well as an urn of coffee, knowing that this was going to be a very long day.

Joanna went directly from the meeting at the Public Safety Building with Miss Foster. She brought with her a briefcase containing stacks of photos and autopsy reports, which included the animal autopsies, as well as the copies of information gleaned from the ME. Arriving at the hotel just minutes after the room service delivery of the breakfast platter, she was pleased with the heavenly aroma of the Columbian brew - an elixir that had kept her going throughout the previous night. Emmett poured and handed her a cup.

Joanna, "Mmmmmm, thank you, (after she sips her coffee she begins). Emmett. I just spoke with the Medical Examiner and I believe that Dr. Hampton may have been murdered using JMV2030. I asked her to have the doctor moved to a different location before the body could be collected and disposed of. He has no family to claim the body, and it has been in storage, but from conversations with the ME, I got the impression that Chuck Delphi gave her orders to list NO cause of death and threatened her to hold the body until he made arrangements for its removal."

Emmett hadn't turned on a television and since he had flown on a private jet, he had not seen the news reports of Dr. Hampton's death. He was shocked when she told him of the death.

Emmett, "You're telling that Dr. Hampton is dead and you are suggesting you believe that Chuck Delphi is involved in the commission of a murder?"

Joanna, "I'm sorry I thought you knew, Dr. Hampton's death was all over the news. What the ME report indicated was that the doctor was first injected with chloral hydrate, followed by a second injection most probably the JMV2030. The Mickey Finn is confirmed, the JMV2030 does not show up in the blood. But the results of the virus are evidenced in the photos of his autopsied organs."

She began to also show him the information she'd received from Miss Foster.

Now she put in front of Rankin, the Dr. Ellison D. Hampton file that includes the blood tests, and M.E.'s narration of the condition of a variety of internal organs. Though Joanna has seen the images, she and Emmett now reviewed the contents of the files in more detail and both are temporarily speechless at the overwhelming content of material before them.

Emmett called room service and asks for a scanner and printer to be brought to the room as soon as possible while he and Joanna took a break to eat some of the breakfast items on the tray and, of course, consume more coffee. They had agreed it was probably best that they both have sets of this information, and in place of the fact that a murder may have been committed, they might be well to consider a third set of information to be held by some secure third party preferably someone in the RiverMoore facility. Considering that Chuck Delphi may be involved, Emmett didn't believe that the information would be safe with a government entity at this point.

The printer and scanner arrived and the pair went to work making copies and pdf files of the data to be stored on a ScanDisk. By the time this task was completed, it was time for lunch, but they had only scratched the surface in the sorting of this boondoggle, so they ordered lunch to be delivered.

Following the light lunch, Rankin told Joanna that he had issued medical alerts to all medical facilities in Texas last night. These alerts should be in the process of being implemented by now. But Rankin checks with his people in Atlanta, to verify that there have been responses from all hospitals and medical service providers that were notified. Once confirmed by his CDC organization that notifications were received and currently being implemented, he continued to share the contents of the alerts with Joanna.

He had issued the alerts based on the limited information he had at the end of his day yesterday. The instructions were to exercise extreme quarantine protocol when dealing with any flu-like symptoms or sudden onset of catastrophic internal organ failure.

He had not shared the fact that there was a virus at the heart of the problem, only that CDC was involved in isolating the suspect infections in an attempt to identify more information about the unexplained deaths, as they were working to identify the cause.

Rankin, "I have already gotten NSA to open up a secure access channel for all Texas medical providers through which they need to report suspected and new exposures. My Atlanta team will be collecting the information which they will be feeding to me around the clock. Of course, I will share the information with you, Joanna, because it looks like we are the only people at this point that we know can be trusted with the information.

Joanna, after you left the meeting, I tried to discuss with Carver about preparing a media alert, because I believe that if we are going towards an epidemic, the public needs to be advised to take precautions. His response, however, was what I considered to be, vigorously opposed to disseminating to the public this virus is lethal.

He told me he does not want CDC to prepare a media alert and suggested the need for secrecy at this point. I'm the kind of person who prefers transparency if it will encourage proactive response within the medical community and the general public. So I have to say that I was stymied at his rather violent opposition in this path to public dissemination of knowledge."

Joanna, "Well Emmett, I can't say I disagree with you about the media campaign but at the risk of playing devil's advocate, what is shared with the public is probably best limited information. In my opinion, the public needs to know part of the story.

I believe the fact that the virus was created to be used as a bio-weapon is probably not something that should be shared. I think it would start a riot against the government. But the people should be advised of a protocol to get vaccinated against what we know is a virus without sharing what we know about its origin."

There was no debate on the subject of the origin needing to remain private and that the information needed to initially be limited to a specific target area Dallas/Fort Worth. Joanna reiterated what she had brought up in the meeting about the inability of the virus to live outside a human host for only a brief amount of time and as such not prone to epidemic infection as an airborne type of flu would be.

Rankin had not been advised of the intricate details of the virus. She explained to him the reason for the randomizing agent introduction to the virus. The purpose of disguising the virus was to insure possible suspicion of its being an engineered bio-medical weapon.

This knowledge closed a few loops in Rankin's confusion. The lack of commonality he'd discovered in his review of the currently unexplained deaths made more sense now. The random factor was a resolution to that question, but of course, it led to new questions, such as, how to build a computer model to generate projections for anti-virus location needs.

This new knowledge served to answer some of Rankin's questions about the spread of the virus. But it also led to Rankin's question, "Well, if it is not airborne, then how is it being transmitted?"

Joanna, "I haven't figured that out yet Emmett, the doctor was injected with it. And the stack of ME reports shows one commonality. All the Texas catastrophic deaths had indications of recently received vaccination type injections, on their arms."

Rankin, "I'm going to Bearlywoke tomorrow morning. I need to find out how much anti-virus vaccine we have in inventory. We are going to need to get this campaign started and get the people to the medical facilities as soon as possible."

Joanna, "I agree we need to do this, but how do you intend to get people to vaccinations without causing a panic? You are going to have to initially target Dallas/Ft Worth, but we are going to need to be prepared for a rush to receive the vaccine. There is no way to keep a lid on what we are trying to do in Texas. There are no limitations where the media is concerned."

They discussed the fact that they had only recently found out, via the media, that Hampton was dead, yet neither of them had been apprised of this by Director Carver. Joanna suggested that she needed to drive to Fort Worth (SAVIOR Labs) to find what the Doctor Hampton's research data showed to facilitate Rankin's need to do a projection model, rather than putting out a blanket public announcement which will surely cause panic and overwhelm the existing inventory of the anti-virus.

Rankin discouraged her from attempting to go to SAVIOR Labs because he had only an hour earlier gotten approval for the quarantine order to keep data inside the facility secure.

Now that he knows about Dr. Hampton's death, there is the question if it would be crime taped by local law enforcement. But he stated that the quarantine order had come from a D.C. Judge, so he would be able to get past any possible police lines to follow up on her concern for the data inside the laboratory.

He told Joanna that after his trip to Bearlywoke, he would proceed to SAVIOR Labs and get the information there. His highest priority was getting the antivirus inventory before he launched the media campaign. He also wanted to know if RiverMoore would be able to manufacture antivirus once he got the formulae.

The media had claimed 'the possibility of foul play was not ruled out'. Hampton had no family, so from a media perspective, there was 'nothing to see here' leaving them to their quest of finding something controversial to sensationalize.

Of course, there was no question of her ability to manufacture the anti-virus. But she added that the question should be raised at Bearlywoke about that facility's inventory and ability because it had been intended to be the production center for the serums once testing was completed.

He told her of the groups of people he has preparing the PSA's and video warnings to the public with the fictional need for booster vaccinations in advance of a possible new flu strain that the CDC is expecting. He had additionally planned, the medical profession bulletins regarding the distribution of the critical vaccines. Rankin had no intention of telling the citizens there have been a bio-weapon accidentally released on the unsuspecting population. National security was at play here and the need for secrecy was critical as it related to the actual virus.

They agreed that the CDC must promote the need for vaccination against a 'suspected upcoming epidemic', followed by the discussion of the need to convey their advice to the President. The existence of this virus, if not quickly contained, would have to be shared with the heads of states of other countries in advance of a possible pandemic as the world had seen back in 2020. Joanna would probably have little to do with this information being imparted to the president, but if there were questions regarding the virus, Joanna would of course be available to be questioned on the details.

She also advised Rankin of the current location of Dr. Hampton's body and the reason she had made the arrangements for the body to be moved to Houston. She discussed why she had made a judgment call about the body, is that if Dr. Hampton had indeed been murdered, that someone would not want that body to have any subsequent evaluation done on it.

The discussions led to the logistics of a media blitz and if Rankin can ascertain if there is sufficient serum to begin the massive undertaking of nationwide distribution. They agreed that Joanna should work with Bearlywoke to find out how much anti-virus had been manufactured or stored.

If RiverMoore was to supplement the manufacture of antivirus, she was going to need to get the formula from Bearlywoke, if she was denied access to SAVIOR Labs, so she'd better get on to this.

Rankin assured her that if she was denied access, he would have the power to get her what she needed if RiverMoore was going to be required to manufacture antivirus serum.

She needed to get on this while Rankin got the ball rolling on the generation of the media reports, propaganda videos, and PSAs which would get the people to the medical facilities to get their shots. So they agreed it was time for them to part ways and do what each needed to do.

BEARLYWOKE STORAGE – HIGHLAND PARK TEXAS

Bearlywoke Storage Facility is deceptively named (possibly this was planned) by the government agencies in control of it. It is a storage facility only in the most minor way. Its factual use is a manufacturing and packaging facility of serum to be distributed to other storage facilities across the United States.

It's a four-square-mile campus with only two entrances from a busy Texas highway. The west side of the perimeter is a large river lined with high levies to protect against flooding. The rear and east sides are adjacent to hundreds of acres of cotton fields as far as the eye can see. The fact that the government leases this land to cotton farmer's, maybe a convenient coincidence to provide an innocuous disguise for the campus. The complete perimeter is landscaped with rows of Green Ash trees that disguise the many video surveillance cameras. Interspersed with the trees are arboreal plants and hedgerow which are lovely too look at from the road, but purposed to hide the miles of high chain-link fence and razor wire set back to provide the secondary defensive line of site security. The manicured lawns are riddled with ground sensors tied, as with the cameras in the trees, to the massive central security control area in the main complex building. The campus is, as such, hidden in plain view from the public.

Entry into Bearlywoke is, as with any government facility, equipped with bio-sensors including an arsenal of biometric identification devices linked to the multiple levels of security clearances required for the various areas of the compound.

Building A

Building A is the front office building, located one mile inside the perimeter main gate. The main building is not a prize of architecture, but rather a simple stone block building yet tornado and hurricane proof even though Highland Park rarely experienced anything resembling a hurricane. The bulletproof plate glass sliding doors have discreet sliding steel security doors invisible to most, but waiting always for the signal to engage a hair-trigger response to a security breach. It is home to offices and non-bio-hazard laboratories. Laid out like the capital letter I, the front is the central series of offices and of course receiving, numbered S1, S2, S3, etc.

The center corridor and offices flanking either side house Security central. This section numbering is D because it also houses the data center. The offices are numbered D1, D2, D3, etc.

The rear of building A is the L wing. The L wing houses non-hazardous laboratories. The right end Room L1 is the opening to an elevator. The security required to enter L1 is second to none in the country. This elevator lowers to an underground labyrinth and is the entry to a very lethal place. The subterranean levels below Building L are home to a bio-hazard laboratory where JMV2030 is converted to AVBW#D, the serum which is deceptively identified to all except the most secure meeting attendees.

The subterranean recesses of Building A, identified as the LL section, is approximately eight times larger than the underwhelming block Building A and several stories deep below the surface level.

It houses its electric transport carts and a large corridor to Building B which has its elevator capable of supporting the constant stream of transports moving packaged serum to the refrigerated warehouse bays.

The entire Bearlywoke campus has its own powerhouse with backup service to provide uninterruptable security and refrigeration control for section LL and building B.

Building B

One offset entry in building B, the Distribution Warehouse, is designed to accommodate truck shipping and deliveries. The trucks, which ship the AVBW#D to distribution centers in hub cities throughout the United States, enter and depart through this single trucking only entrance.

There are government contracted private security guards at both entrances round the clock. The truck entrance is wide enough for single trucks passing through. It is equipped with state of the art electronically controlled gates and barrier rods that rise from deep in the ground in the event of an emergency.

Building C

Housing the Motor Pool and mechanical plant are Building C. Next to Building B, located two miles from the highway entry gate closest to the riverside of the property, is the maintenance garage with a staff of mechanics and equipment to ensure that any mal-functioning transport will not impact the movement of the precious cargo being manufactured and distributed.

TEMPORARY FORT WORTH FIELD OFFICE

Now that Rankin had been in extensive communications with Joanna Moore at his Marriott field office, he would be demanding to know how much anti-virus is stored at Bearlywoke and how long it takes to manufacture. Dr. Yīshēng gave him no response to the question over the phone. This was critical for him to prepare his demographic targeting of PSAs. He knew, of course, that the medical community will need to be advised nationwide and he didn't plan to accept a dodge when he asked the question, face to face, with Dr. Yīshēng. The doctor had attempted to deceive in their phone conversation, by stating that the virus was not ready for prime time human testing.

From the new temporary office, Rankin made arrangements to meet with Dr. Yīshēng at Bearlywoke first thing in the morning.

After a tour through the very secure complex Building A, Doctor Yīshēng continued explaining to Rankin that there are two different strains of the anti-virus identified suffixes AVBW#D & AVBW#S. His explanation for the need for two different anti-virus serums was a practiced lie. The doctor indicated that genetic markers dictated the need for specific serum; as such the administering of the correct AVBW# was critical to successful inoculations.

This reference to genetic markers set alarms ringing in Rankin's head. Yes, all humans had identifiable genetic markers that made them prone to certain medical maladies, but the suggestion that the entire population was genetically cataloged was empirically preposterous.

For example, Emmett knew that human testing had not begun and if the virus was truly designed to target humans of another country and culture, the anti-virus couldn't have been limited to only two serum types. The doctor's story about two vaccines was a complete fabrication, and Rankin knew it!

At this critical time, however, his mission of getting anti-virus to the masses was more important than debating about the reason for this alarm bell ringing in his head. Dr. Yīshēng wasn't aware that Mr. Rankin, was also an accomplished doctor with specific experience in the study of virology, but this oversight was best left uncorrected since Yīshēng was ill-advised, rude, or being deceptive. If this genetic marker reference was deliberate, the underlying reason could be subterfuge, and as such very unsettling.

Yīshēng continued to advise Rankin that in addition to informing the public, the more important communication would be the dissemination to the medical community that its adherence to the use of the proper ID#s was critical. The Doctor Yīshēng continued to stress that Rankin should develop and implement the use of a special website, hosted and maintained by the NSA, which could provide the census and coordinated data for accuracy in this dosing protocol. This belaboring of the ID#s was annoying but unfortunately, Rankin let it go as his immediate need was more pressing.

Rankin had his people in DC scouring the medical

records for deaths that occurred with speedy but catastrophic physiological anomalies.

His DC staff was extremely competent and Rankin knew that when he returned to his office, there would be volumes of information, charts, and graphs to help him with his demographic targeting.

Rankin was not advised, during his tour, about the L wing of Building A with its subterranean annex and an underground tunnel connecting the packaging lab to the warehouse Building B, nor was he given a tour of the Building B that was a hive of distribution activity of materials that Dr. Yīshēng had claimed were not in existence at this time.

Dr. Yīshēng claimed there were 1000 units of anti-virus vaccine of the three serum types. This wasn't the greatest news for Rankin. He didn't know yet that this was another less than candid report from Dr. Yīshēng. And he hadn't been privileged to see the actual laboratory, manufacturing, and distribution locations that had much more serum than reported.

DECOMMISSIONED

TERRY ANGEL

The Director of Bearlywoke is Doctor Yīshēng, born in Beijing, China. He had studied around the world, including degrees with Oxford Business, Stanford Medical, and Harvard Medical. His list of medical and viral studies was second to none. There are volumes of research papers and publications as well as keynote speeches at symposiums around the world that bear his name. His directorship at the Bearlywoke DOD storage facility was not high profile or particularly prestigious by comparison to the rest of his resume, but his work at Bearlywoke was designed to meet his personal target goal which extended far beyond the United States of America.

Dr. Yīshēng's assistant is Terry Angel, a Stanford educated microbiologist. Terry's knowledge and experience pale when put beside Yīshēng, but he had selected her for her loyalty. His need for the unfailing loyalty of his staff was critical to his goals.

Terry's loyalty has never been challenged and had been much rewarded. Dr. Yīshēng had given her nearly unlimited responsibility for more than 10 years but today she is struggling with whether this loyalty has been misplaced.

Reports have been coming in from the data center with lists of deaths – unexplained deaths with descriptions of symptoms that resemble those caused by the JMV2030 military virus housed here in Bearlywoke. The reports were designated to be delivered to Yīshēng, but Terry collected them up, with the intent of screening the information, as prioritization was one of her strengths.

She had, over the years, saved Yīshēng a lot of time by delegating things that he shouldn't have to be bothered with, so today was just another of those days until she saw the content of these reports. Dr. Yīshēng has not mentioned these deaths and this omission in communication is not characteristic of their relationship. She was reluctant to ask him for details or express her concern whether there was indeed a relationship between JMV2030 and the unexplained deaths in the greater Dallas Fort Worth area hospitals as evidenced in these reports. She didn't want to challenge him, as he was her superior, but these death statistics seemed alarming to her.

She had spoken with Joanna Moore at RiverMoore a few times over the past year, mostly regarding expedition of shipments from RiverMoore to Bearlywoke. Terry pondered and finally decided she must take action by contacting Joanna who might be the person to reach out to with her concerns. It is, after all, a RiverMoore virus that is being housed here. And these reports seem to indicate a relationship between the virus and the locale of the deaths.

There also seems to have been an arduous amount of activity in development section LL (subterranean level biohazard labs and manufacturing) where the anti-virus products (AVBW#D, AVBW#G, and AVBW#S) are being packaged for distribution to other DOD storage locations across the USA. This could indicate that Dr. Y knew about the virus being disseminated to the public and another reason why she felt compelled to speak to someone outside Bearlywoke about her concerns.

Since the anti-virus products were intended for military applications on non-U.S. soil, it would seem that the storage locations should be located near military bases, particularly Air Force as that would be the means for shipping to the international receiving locations. Terry was able to put aside her loyalty for the doctor until she was able to gather facts to dispel her concerns.

It hadn't occurred to her to look at the shipment locations being on or near military bases. But now, she looked at distribution bills of lading and discovered her suspicions were well-founded. The storage facilities receiving the deliveries did not seem to be on or near any Air Force bases. The trucks were delivering to civilian storage locations near some very large urban population hubs.

She made a mental note of this, to mention in addition to the Bearlywoke renaming of the serums. Terry had no idea why the serums were renamed, but it was information that may be of interest to Joanna Moore. Following is what Bearlywoke houses renamed, manufactured, and packaged for distribution:

JMV2030 = JMV2030 - Original bio-weapon

No changes to the name as it is the base product and not distributed to any facility other than SAVIOR Labs.

AVBW#D = JMV2030_R - Randomized bio-weapon

AVBW#G = AV_JMV2030 - Anti-virus to the bio-weapon (Government use only)

AVBW#S = Additional – Bearlywoke product, placebo

Terry did not have any idea how the #D rename corresponded to the randomized agent or why it was preceded by AV (anti-virus designation – was this a labeling error?). Nor did she have any idea what the #S designation represented. Since she seemed to be out of the circle of confidence with Dr. Yīshēng, she didn't think it was a good idea to ask questions about this. But she was hoping that perhaps Ms. Moore would be able to sort it out.

Dr. Hampton never knew that the serum #D and # S were already being manufactured, packaged, and distributed in advance of his testing completion. The packaging for AVBW#D, AVBW#S, and AVBW#G are liquid serum to be injected as any normal vaccination, booster shot, or flu vaccine.

Terry used her cell to make a call to her friend, Cool Mann.

Cool looks like someone out of a time machine, his hair is the largest mass of dreads she had ever seen. His arms and neck are covered completely with tattoos to coordinate with the tribal holes in his ears and piercings of his face. He had an attitude to match his weird presence, but they had mutual respect because she didn't judge people for their idiosyncrasies. Cool sure had plenty of them!

Terry had been pizza bar buddies with Cool since Stanford. She had met him at an off-campus watering hole that served pizza by the slice and a variety of local microbrews.

He was working his way through college by serving pizza and pool hustling in his off time. They dated as many college friends date, just time to hang out and get away from studies. Not long after she finished school, she got the opportunity to follow Dr. Yīshēng and assist him at the Bearlywoke Storage location in Texas.

Cool was still, after graduation, serving slices of pizza, while each of them mourned Terry's impending departure. Just a week away from her move, while sharing a bottle of tequila, she shared the great news with him. She told him happily that she had spoken with Dr. Yīshēng and got his permission to hire Cool to work in the warehousing area of the facility. Terry had fabricated and submitted a resume to the doctor, who accepted her offer based on his desire to ensure that she went to Texas. If Terry trusted this person with the strange name, that was enough for the doctor. He warned her that if Mr. Mann didn't work out, she would have to be the person to terminate him. Of course, she agreed and promised happily that all things would be just fine. And so it went that Cool also moved to a small Texas apartment near the complex that Terry lived in.

"Cool!" says Terry from the privacy of the ladies' washroom, "I've got something going on that requires something special from my special guy………."

Cool, "What can I do for my favorite Angel?"

Terry, "I need samples of AVBW#D and #G and #S. I know, I know – it's secure and all – but something is going on and I need to have another set of eyes to look into it. On the QT, Cool."

Cool, "Do I sense a conspiracy, pretty Angel?"

Terry, "Yes possibly, something I need to verify. Can you put them in my car in a little cold pack?"

Cool, "You got it sweetie – can we touch base tomorrow night so you can enlighten me?"

Terry, "Will do Cool thanks – I owe you! Your place, I'll bring the tequila!"

Cool, "Be careful my Angel, you know this is nasty stuff."

Terry takes an unusual lunch off-site this day and delivers the precious cold packed items to Joanna at RiverMoore and they made arrangements to talk later. Joanna tasks Terry with the extraction of information on the quantities of available serum in Bearlywoke. Before Terry leaves, she remembers to give Joanna the printout of the distribution hubs. "Strange, she said, they don't seem to be near big military bases…"

They agree to meet again once Joanna has had the

opportunity to have the samples evaluated. Joanna promises to escalate the testing of the samples before their meeting the following morning. Terry returned to work to collect as much distribution and inventory information as possible to share with Joanna.

JOSHUA'S HOUSE

Using the partially downloaded schematics that Beth had located, Josh was able to determine the steps necessary to begin the MSA's recommission process. The first item was a communications cable to link the droid's comm port to Josh's laptop. By spicing the two cables from his parts inventory, Josh managed to get that done quickly.

The second part of the process was a restart of the primary power source. The manner of connection of the power source and voltage needed making bypassing it too cumbersome if not impossible without special equipment. That meant the existing power source, which was fully intact, just needed a restart pulse. Unfortunately, that required a properly timed energy pulse of sufficient voltage to kick-in the power source's internal reactor.

While Josh was agonizing over the options for a power source restart, Beth in her growing frustration, called out to him. "Josh, I can't get any search results to come back on to the Doctor, or SAVIOR Labs, or MSA. It's like I'm being blocked! I can search for cute shoes and stuff, but no Doctor. Any ideas?"

Without losing his focus on the droid, Josh drags his

hands through his short curls as he tersely responds, "Beth, I am trying to figure out how to jumpstart this droid's main power module, which is, a slightly larger issue than your shoe shopping…. Now if you don't mind………."

Her response was calm despite his self-involved comment. "What do you need to get that done – the jumpstart I mean."

Josh nearly sputtered from his frustration. "What I need is a short pulse of high voltage. Is that in your search list of things to do???"

Without a heart tick of time, Beth says – "How about a Taser – or defibrillator?"

He stared at her, he'd been struggling for an hour and she pulls the perfect solution like a rabbit from a hat!

"Try using the VPN," said Joshua.

"What?" said Beth, "What has VPN to do with a power supply?"

"For your searching, Beth", said the now humbled Josh.

Beth had used the virtual private network in the past but only when she did searches that she wanted to be anonymous. She launched the VPN application and when it notified her that a private connection was established, she relaunched her search and got some hits.

"Thanks, Josh, you are a genius - that worked!"

Josh just smiled.

* * *

Utah

At the Utah facility, the analyst noted the VPN connection on the Trace App Log.

"Smart move buddy, but no prize for you – I already got you!" The analyst entered another few commands and a window appeared on his monitor. On the left was a progress bar going from 0 to 100 left to right and the right pane was a window containing streams of flowing characters. The target computers' memory and storage contents were being downloaded and analyzed.

A minute later, just as a matter of ego, he clicked a button on the app. "Just want you to know you aren't alone Joshua Klein", he chuckles.

* * *

Beth exclaimed, "What the heck is this?" as a similar set of windows opened on her monitor. Only these had a progress bar going from 100 to 0 left to right in the windowpane. Josh walked over to have a look. What he saw was the progress bar at 85 percent and shrinking fast.

"Oh SHIT!" he exclaimed as he pulled the computer's power cord from the wall outlet, unfortunately too late.

Beth, "What just happened?"

Josh, "We've been hacked. And whoever it was got most of our data from the computer."

Beth, "OH SHIT!" cried Beth as her hands went into her wild red curls, as though she could find some solution hiding in there.

Josh, "I'm so sorry Beth."

Beth, "Sorry for what?"

Josh sadly, "That I missed the risk we took with this droid. The message we got from it, the blocked search results, and now this. I think someone is looking for us."

Beth, "So you think this is related to the MSA?"

Josh, "I don't know, but all these years of shopping, and now this - seems too coincidental. I think we should go somewhere safer, somewhere we're harder to find until we're sure it's not a problem."

Beth, "Ok, where?"

Josh, "I have the storage unit out in Decatur. I paid cash in advance for it and used a different name – just in case. Let's grab what we can with MSA and hit the road. Do we have any portable food – like some peanut butter and bread?"

Beth, "Right, I can do that."

While Josh loads MSA into the car, Beth loads up some parts boxes, cables, modules, power module tools, and a flashlight. She then grabs some sodas a loaf of bread, a jar of peanut butter and jelly, and off they go.

* * *

Utah

In Utah, the NSA analyst clapped his hands together and let out a raucous "BOOM!" The AI of the app had already begun returning results. He placed a call to Stephanie Wolff as previously instructed.

"Director Wolff, this is Dave Tillis. I have information for you on that special project."

"Go ahead, replies Stephanie, tell me what you have."

While he talks, he is compiling an email with a summary. "I've got names and addresses, pictures, SSN, social media info, and lots more."

"So who are we talking about?" asks Stephanie.

Dave, "Joshua Klein and Beth McCallum both at 1483 Glenoak, Dallas Texas. Want to know her dress size?"

Stephanie Wolff, "No, just name, address, and pictures first then send me a detailed report of everything you've found – employment records, etc. Also, keep on these two, and watch for any other activity."

"Yes, ma'am," and Dave hangs up to finish the email summary which he sends to Director Wolff. Moments later, Stephanie receives the email, reviews the contents, and forwards it to Michael Carver over at the FBI. Within minutes of receiving the Wolff email, Michael Carver initiates a nationwide APB on Joshua Klein and Elizabeth McCallum, of Dallas Texas.

DECATUR

On the way to the storage facility, Josh and Beth make two stops. The first is at West Dallas Hospital. Josh parks several rows back from the emergency entrance under a tree planted in the divider that separates the drive and the parking lot. They wait without speaking.

MSA is blinking but Josh and Beth did not notice. *Human has tools, human has ignition coil*, is the message MSA is trying to convey.

After twenty minutes, that seemed like an eternity, flashing lights appear entering the emergency driveway and approach the hospital ER entrance. Josh steps out of the car and dons a baseball cap followed by pulling the hood of his jacket over it. He moves slowly toward the ambulance. The EMTs throw open the rear doors of the ambulance and remove the patient transport quickly to the emergency entrance with the waiting Triage team. Beth had coached Josh in the techniques of the paramedics and he knew they would be gone for several minutes – there would be paperwork inside including patient handoff and retrieval of their ambulance equipment as they processed the admission of the patient to the ER triage team.

Josh reaches the ambulance and steps into the back. After about 15 seconds, he spots a door labeled D-Fib and opens it to reveal a case. After removing the case he pops the catch and verifies it is a defibrillator which he then re-latched.

He hops out of the ambulance and slips around the passenger side of the ambulance and heads toward Beth and the car keeping the ambulance between him and the emergency room doors as long as possible. The entire caper took less than 60 seconds.

Back at the car, he puts the case on the back seat floor. Beth remarks in a whisper, "Wow you're like a pro at this!" and Josh replies with a smile. "My heart is pounding! You might need to use this on me!"

They pulled slowly out of the parking lot and head for their second stop. Westbound down the highway is a rest area with fuel and food.

Josh entered into the parking lot of a fast-food restaurant so Beth can grab a quick meal as they had not eaten, with all the excitement of the MSA droids message and the hacking of Josh's PC. The food they had brought with them would serve them better later.

The place is empty except for the counter clerk and another in the prep area. At the counter, she orders a couple of burgers and a soda. The clerk takes her money and hands her a cup for the soda. She turns toward the fountain to fill her cup and spots the news broadcast on the flat screen in the dining area. She freezes in place as she stares at photos of herself and Josh, driver license photos, showing on the screen in living color. She could not hear the news anchor, but read the closed- captioning persons of interest in the possible murder of a local doctor, Doctor Ellison D Hampton– call 1800FBICRIME.

A moment later the clerk, with Beth's bagged order, in his hand, called out "Miss." Beth, still frozen in place does not respond. Again, the clerk calls out, "Miss," and then a few seconds later with a louder tone, "Ma'am!" At which time Beth turns toward the counter, "your order," and he holds out the bag. Beth looks at the bag, hesitates, and then snatches it quickly and dashes out of the restaurant.

"Weirdo," mumbled the clerk.

No one in the restaurant connects her to the news item. The screen is difficult to see from behind the counter, and the limited number of employees weren't interested in the news anyway. As she climbs into the car and slams the door with a bag in hand, Josh spies the empty cup and notices Beth staring out the front windshield. "Beth?" No response. He then notices her hands are shaking. He jostles her arm and in a slow voice calls her name again to get her attention "BETH!"

Slowly she turns to look at Josh. As he carefully removes the sunglasses she is wearing he sees she has tears in her eyes. "What the heck is wrong?" he asks.

After a moment, she sucks in a breath and said: "We are persons of interest..."

Josh, "Person interested in what?"

"PERSONS OF INTEREST IN A DOCTOR'S MURDER JOSH, the doctor that had MSA, the doctor from SAVIOR Labs" replied Beth. "I saw it on the news in there!"

He turns back and faces forward. "Shit, shit, shit!"

Beth asks "Josh, what are we going to do?" as she begins to sob.

"First off we are getting outta here, the storage locker is the safest place right now." With that, he backs out of their parking spot and takes off for Decatur.

Once at the facility Josh stops the car outside the building that houses his unit. He looks at Beth who has been silent except for the sobs since they left the restaurant. She had finally stopped crying a couple of miles back.

Josh, "Are you ok?"

Beth, "What are we going to do?"

Josh, "I don't quite know yet Beth – we'll figure out something. Maybe we turn ourselves in."

Beth, "We need to know what the droid meant by 'Must save Mankind' first."

Josh, "Let's get this stuff moved into my locker and then we can think this through."

Beth can only follow – her brain is in a fog and a sort of robotic walk is about all she can manage, so Josh places simple things in her hands to carry.

The storage facility was a retired egg farm. The long buildings had been converted to rows of 6' x 12' storage lockers with 3- 1/2 foot steel commercial doors, each with a handle and deadbolt. Security consisted of a barbed wire-topped chain-link fence around the perimeter and closed-circuit cameras that had stopped working years ago.

Once they had the boxes and droid in the locker, Josh moved the car to a place amongst some old silos and tossed a smelly canvas tarp over the back of it to camouflage the car.

When Josh returned to the locker he shuts and door and latched the deadbolt. The single light is barely adequate to illuminate the whole area, but he can see Beth standing in the middle of the boxes he had stacked along the walls. He walks up to her thinking about what to say and once in front of her he says, "Beth...."

Her response was to throw her arms around him and start to sob again. At first, he stands with arms outstretched but then wraps one around while the other followed suit pulling her tight to protect her from her pain.

"I'm so sorry that I got you into this Beth", says Joshua. Beth responds, "Josh, I chose to do this, we've been a team and teams don't just drop the ball because the streetlights come on. We can do this if we can work together, right? I need you to tell me it is gonna be ok, I've never been so afraid in my life!" He couldn't say that, but he could continue to hold her tightly.

After eating the now cold burgers, Beth had recovered herself enough to try to collaborate with him on what their next steps needed to be. Josh stated the obvious, that they are going to need a better location to recommission the droid as the storage locker is so full of boxes, there is barely enough room to move about not to mention the inadequate power they would need to restart MSA's power unit.

Beth offers a plan, "Let's try SAVIOR Labs that is where MSA was working. We need to try to find a connection to Dr. Hampton. If we supposedly killed a doctor, we should find out why he would need killing and why we would be persons of interest..........Josh, why are they connecting us to a dead doctor? Oh crap – never mind. 'Cause someone tracked our search for MSA schematics, right? I just don't get why the government is concerned about a relatively antiquated model droid. I think we need to find out more about SAVIOR Labs if we are going to find the answers to our questions."

Throughout the conversation, the MSA's eyes are blinking furiously attempting to send them messages that they were too preoccupied to notice.

DR. HAMPTON – DECOMMISSIONED
MUST RECOMMISSION MSA121068
MSA HAS TOOLS
MUST SAVE MANKIND

Josh, "I don't know Beth a lot of damage has been done. We are now fugitives of the federal government – guilty until proven innocent if the FBI is involved. We are going to have to be careful Beth. I blame myself – I got so excited about an operational droid and decoding the message, I just didn't even slightly consider this kind of risk. Besides, how are we going to get into SAVIOR Labs now? If the doctor was murdered there, it would probably be locked down as a crime scene."

Beth says, "What about the droid, it should know how to get us in there."

Joshua, "That's very astute but we're going to need more space to do the recommission – it's too cramped here and who knows how reliable the single power outlet is. I think it is too risky to try that here. With one outlet, we could blow the power, so we can't risk trying a one-shot solution."

MSA's eyes are blinking like a White House Christmas tree but they don't notice – MSA is blinking:

JUMPER CABLES – HUMANS HAVE TOOLS

Beth pulls yet another rabbit out of the hat. "How about a model home like they put in the new suburbs they are building everywhere? They have real estate people during the day – showing the models and trying to sell the lots to build on! But they only show them in the day. This late at night, they will be empty. They have lights and power."

"How do you do that?" asked the amazed Josh, "Pull a rabbit from a hat!"

Beth, "Do what?"

Josh, "Never mind, find us with a new subdivision with no neighbors. We need to take a little road trip. MSA is going to have to stay put for a little bit."

Beth, "Okie Dokie coach! We can do this."

On the way back to the little fast food place, Josh explains that they are going to need to get near a WIFI location, so Beth can search the real estate ads for an open house.

Her search for models specifically targeted between Decatur and Highland Park (SAVIOR Labs location) – it must be a house with all electric utilities. Furnished would sure be a bonus. The model homes would be sparsely furnished, but there might even be beds in the bedrooms of a nice model. Josh continued to pour over the partial schematics. Euless was on the way to SAVIOR Labs and pretty spread out, but there were several new subdivisions listed with models. Many were showing the surrounding lots yet to be built on, at least according to the maps. She bookmarked multiple location listings just in case.

DECOMMISSIONED

FOOTE AND MOUSE – FBI FIELD AGENTS

"Crap on a cracker," says FBI field agent Adrian Mouse. Mouse hands her phone to Foote who sees a text message from Stephanie Wolff at the NSA:

"West Dallas hospital - emergency vehicle robbed – single item: defibrillator. YOUR SUSPECTS - FIND THEM!"

Foote, "I'm confused we are chasing two persons of interest in a possible murder right?"

Mouse, "Right"

Foote, "So what does this have to do with a defib machine?"

Mouse, "No idea but when NSA sends an order to the FBI, we need to jump."

Adrian Mouse is 5'9" with a military haircut and physique to match. Her partner has been trying for a year to get her to change her look, so she had recently agreed to an image modification to include a tuft of blue bang on her forehead. The field office team had laughed themselves silly and even brought in cupcakes covered in chocolate icing with tufts of blue strands resembling the new hair. But Foote hadn't laughed, he'd been her teammate for eight years and they would each lay down their respective lives for the other. He jokingly referred to the tuft as "her tail' but it didn't offend Mouse when he said it. If she would ever be attracted to a guy – Dave Foote would be the one, not because of his scrupulously trimmed hair and clean-shaven babyface, but simply because he was nice and trustworthy. The field office team laughed about the pairing of Foote and Mouse. They were often referred to as "the foot and mouth disease team."

The true reason for this mission has remained undisclosed to 'the disease team' as it was above their pay grade. Their orders were to search for Klein and McCallum who were persons of interest in a possible murder of a doctor and they must have a droid with them based on the little information fed to them. Working with the NSA was not unheard of and neither was working with Stephanie Wolff.

Stephanie Wolff is located in the Bluffdale, Utah NSA office, but her reputation throughout government agencies is well known. A message from Stephanie Wolff is like getting a ticket to the 50-yard line at the Super Bowl. Stephanie Wolff is the stuff dreams are made of – she is hot hot – but colder than dry ice. Dream-on people– you touch her, you get frostbite.

Miss Wolff will never be accused of sleeping her way to the top. She is probably the smartest woman on the planet – that's just not fair thinks Foote, The God that put her on the planet had a cruel sense of humor – to make such a perfect specimen of desire then put Freon rather than blood in her veins and the worst thing – to make her smart.

When Foote and Mouse get an order from her it's a double-edged sword – one side to dream about the hottest female in the U.S. government and the other is the icy fear of the consequences of failure.

Foote, "So where does the Ice Queen think we need to look for a stolen defib machine and a couple of hackers? It seems like something big is happening – peeps are tense – but a defib and a couple of college geeks? Just doesn't seem like something the Ice Queen would bother with."

Mouse, "Oh she sent a follow-up: Hospital – Stephens Park Hospital – Colorado Blvd."

They were aware of the APB on Klein and McCallum but that hardly seems like an FBI mission, but what's the big deal about a stolen defibrillator? A possible murder ok – maybe – high profile – but these aren't even murder suspects – just persons of interest in a possible murder and defibrillator theft?

DECOMMISSIONED

RECOMMISSION EULESS TEXAS

The model home was locked with one of those lockbox devices which have three numbers to dial to open the key panel. People put the key in them when they lock up, but they never bother to spin the three dials. *DUH*, thinks Josh *all I have to do is spin the dials around one time back to the numbers showing when it was closed.* And just like that – they were in.

MSA is now lying on top of a dining table in the real estate developers' newly featured model home.

Josh, "MSA – I don't know if you are still receiving me – but if you are – hang in there – we are about to jump-start your power supply. This is gonna hurt you more than me.."

MSA, One blink (*yes*)

Beth, "Josh, this is no time for levity – we don't know how long we can be safe here you didn't see that television with our pictures. I never heard of that Doctor before we found MSA, but now our pictures are plastered all over hells' half acre with a finder's fee. We need to get MSA operational so we can find out what we are running from."

Josh, "Ladies STARRRRT YOUR ….. ENGINES !!!!!" (defib THUMP – MSA's body jumps) "nope – hit it again Beth" THUMP - slight smell of singed plastic. "One more time Beth !"

MSA: "NO!!!!"

MSA's power supply is slightly smoking but it has a voice now. Josh is astounded, "It worked! I can't believe it worked! Uh oh!!!" Joshua rushes to get a fire extinguisher in case the adage about 'where there's smoke there is fire' could be true.

The rising smoke has triggered a fire alarm – no flames – but the alarm is loud and unending. Beth asks, "Can you walk MSA – or better yet – can you run?" MSA responds, "Yes MSA can run", it isn't pretty - but it runs. "WAIT, WAIT human - remove tracking!"

What Josh and Beth did not know is that the recommission also restarted the GPS circuit in MSA, whoever put that GPS tracker in MSA did not intend for the droid to disappear and it wouldn't take long to triangulate on it.

Neither Josh nor Beth connected what MSA was trying to convey. Even if they had understood what MSA was attempting to warn them off, they couldn't risk trying to figure out how to shut off the tracker right now – the Fire Department would be here soon.

NSA MONITORING DIVISION FORT WILLIAMS

Online monitor contacts Dave Tillis.

Beau Clark, "Hey Dave, this is weird. I'm getting' a GPS tracker signal – code red, y'all got a tracker list? Can't think the last time I saw a code red signal tracker alert."

Dave, "Yeah – I've got one here somewhere, what's the tracker number?"

Beau, "hmmm DOD MSAPROJ-CLEARCUT- watt on God's green earth is Clearcut?"

Dave, "Says it's a droid – MSA droid – security clearance needed for more info. Thanks for letting me know – I'll call Miss Wolff – I think this is an FBI mission."

Beau, "The code is DOD – why do you say FBI?"

Dave, "Anything DOD goes to FBI – I guess that is Stephanie's chain of command. I'm not gonna question it, just let her know and she will handle it through the proper channels."

Beau calls Stephanie Wolff's office and left a message suggesting that the DOD tracker is out of his paygrade but DOD might want to check their tracker data. But she also got a call from the analyst, Dave Tillis – just in case...

Stephanie gets the message and she is immediately seething as Carver is losing his mind. The droid is on the move, it has been recommissioned!!!

The conveyance of information between numerous government agencies is great for Joshua and Beth because the time involved in passing the buck up the chain of command to Carver and Delphi gave them a slight advantage. The fact that Delphi was inebriated from all that scotch on an empty stomach was a bonus because the information would probably sit until the morning.

WALMART

Now that MSA is mobile, they need clothes – disguises as it were – MSA needs to be disguised in some way – but since it was a model home there was no clothing. Beth was going to have to think of another way to disguise MSA once they got away from here. She is thinking that they need to find a laundromat to snag some clothes from a dryer once they get away from Euless. But MSA had a better solution.

Joshua, "Beth, we've gotta get rid of this car and my phone – and I need to get a couple 'use it and toss it' phones – they must have gotten my address so the lap and phone can't be turned on now. He had pulled the batteries out while in the storage facility to ensure they couldn't be tracked through the GPS systems of those items.

"Agreed", says Beth, "and I need to get us some clothes MSA must look more domestic – they are looking for an MSA right?"

MSA, "I have tools – I am GPS"

Joshua, "We don't need tools MSA – we need WIFI and a vehicle."

MSA, "MSA has tools – Walmart please"

Joshua, "Okie Dokie, Walmart it is."

Inside Walmart – Beth goes and grabs clothing, hair color, hats, and a scarf to cover MSA's bald head. Joshua goes to pick up a couple of disposable phones and they had agreed to meet at the front cashier area – self-checkout.

Electronics clerk, "After you pay for 'em, bring 'em back with the receipt and I will activate 'em for you." Joshua looks at MSA – MSA's eyes blink - 01101001 00100000 01101000 01100001 01110110 01100101 00100000 01110100 01101111 01101111 01101100 01110011 (*I have tools*). Joshua, "Ok thanks – we'll be back in a couple of minutes.' On the way to the self-checkout, he tells the droid, "MSA, I can't read binary that fast can we just use one blink for yes and two for no?" MSA – one blink.

At the self-check, Joshua scans their purchases – payment method dialog shows on the screen, MSA puts its hand in front of the scanner – dialog screen shows – "Do you want cashback?" MSA looks at Joshua - one blink. Joshua says, "Yes MSA that will be nice." The machine begins to spit out currency – lots of it – not the $20 on the screen – but stacks of $20 bills. "STOP", whispers Joshua, "we don't want to draw attention!"

Once inside the car, Joshua hands the phones to MSA, Do you have the tool to activate? MSA, "Yes, MSA has tools." MSA scans the phones activating each with 50K minutes. Joshua, "SWEET MSA. I'm gonna like having you around!" MSA, "Yes MSA has tools. MSA has GPS."

"Beth, please count this money – we're gonna go buy a new ride and put some miles between us and this Walmart – they have security cameras everywhere." Beth quickly counts the cash – "$4480, well it should get us a very well used old van – we need something to haul stuff in." MSA looks at Joshua, "Joshua need more?" Joshua mentally debates, *MSA is our golden goose!* "Naaaaa maybe later Goose.

We need to get to SAVIOR Labs and find out what happened to the Doctor."

Goose, "`Doctor decommissioned – MSA has GPS. Joshua?`"

webster Dictionary:

   Goose 1. any of numerous large waterfowl (family Anatidae) that are intermediate between the swans and ducks and have long necks, feathered lores, and reticulate tarsi

   Goose 2. a poke between the buttocks

Goose again, "`Joshua, Goose has other meanings? Goose has GPS.`"

Joshua, "Goose, do you know a safe place where we can investigate the Doctor's decommission? Is that why you keep mentioning that you have GPS?"

Goose, "`Yes, No.`"

Joshua, "Oh wait – I asked you two questions let me try again Do you know a safe place to investigate decommission?"

Goose, "`Yes.`"

Joshua, "Is your reference to GPS related to investigating the doctor?"

Goose, "`NO – MSA has GPS – Agents track GPS – must remove.`"

Joshua, "WHAT? You are equipped with GPS tracking?"

Goose, "`Yes must remove.Human has tools?`"

Joshua, "Crap – can you give me a clue how to disable?"

Goose, "`Yes.`"

Joshua, "Goose, we need to work on our communication skills."

Goos, "`Yes, communication, Joshua, Other meaning for Goose?`"

Joshua, "Oh, Golden Goose - a term of endearment and

friendship."

Goose: "Thank you, Joshua Goose."

Joshua only thought for a second whether he should clarify this miscommunication, but decided they didn't have time right now.

It is dry in north Texas now so when Josh spots a large drainage culvert between the freeway and the feeder road, he quickly gets onto the feeder and pulls the car into the culvert. This should shield the GPS signal until he can get it disabled. Beth finds a cool spot to act as a lookout. The disabling of the GPS didn't take long. With Goose coaching, Josh isolates the circuit number that powers the GPS.

* * *

Utah

Just about this same time the DOD Clearcut tracker stops tracking. Beau, at NSA, begins to bang on his computer furiously, hoping beyond hope that it is a computer malfunction. He'd been monitoring the code red GPS tracker for about an hour.

"I sure 'nuff don't like messing with the DOD voodoo spooks but if the signal is lost, they sure as hell gonna blame me", thinks Beau. Alas, no amount of pounding or refreshing yields the tracker signal. Stephanie Wolff is gonna have to make yet another urgent call – this one is going to be much more contentious. Beau picks up his desk phone.

Stephanie Wolff, "ARE YOU ABSOLUTELY SURE? DOD trackers don't just shut off – not this one! I'll be right there."

With the beautiful Ms. Wolff looking over his shoulder at his playback of the tracker monitoring –intently watching the timestamps she is getting colder by the second it seems. Beau, "I'm almighty sorry ma'am but the signal just stopped liken a deer in headlights on a foggy night, Miss Wolff ma'am."

Beau was born a Ragin Cajun and when Miss Wolff was around, his drawl was more pronounced. It seemed to calm her like sippin' sweet tea on the porch. But the Cajun charm doesn't work today – she has turned into the Ice Queen. Beau needs to stay under the radar now – *don't wanna get me frostbite*, thinks Beau.

Stephanie Wolff quickly leaves to go call DOD Roger Ackinsen. It almost seems like the room is colder as she departs, like an open window on a Utah winter night, so frigid is her draft.

ON THE ROAD AGAIN

Josh, "Ok Beth, we are off the grid now. Next stop, Cars R Us."

Josh and Beth didn't get out of the car before Smilin' Sam Putnam races out of the office to vigorously pump the hands of both Josh and Beth.

"How y'all doing today? What beauty you lookin' for? Fuel economy? Go to work, family car?? You want it, Cars R Us got it. Didn't catch your names…"

Josh and Beth quickly identified themselves as brother and sister, Danny and Barb Jones. "Thanks, Sam. We're looking for a second vehicle, older model maybe a van or SUV."

"You want it, we got it!" exclaims Smilin' Sam Putnam. He quickly steers them to the most expensive shiny SUV on the lot.

"Well' says Beth, "that is lovely but I was thinking of something a bit older, we just need to haul soccer equipment for the nieces, perhaps something a little more affordable. I was planning on paying cash."

CASH??? Cha-Ching!!! Sam likes the sound of that – he has a way of skimming a bit for himself when cash is involved.

"Alrighty, I've got a sturdy van – let me get the keys."

Josh is already heading for the ugly van. They had Goose stashed a block away in the parking lot of a 'for sale' antique store. Beth hands the keys to Joshua's car to Sam, could you hold onto our car while we take this for a little test drive – just around the block. Cash talks, thinks Sam.

Off they go – one block to the 'for sale' antique store. Josh opens the hood and Goose does whatever it is he does with his 'tools' and the van is now purring like a longhaired cat on a winter night and they're off again to Cars R Us.

Beth negotiates a deal for the very unattractive van for the low, low price today only $3899.99 – they have instore financing for poor credit. Keep the change thinks Josh as Beth peels off the cash. They get a quick bill of sale – for the AS-IS – no warranty implied sale. Smilin' Sam will be happy to fill in the selling price later if they have to get going to soccer practice.

The van and car drive off. Beth picks up Goose in the van and follows Josh to the nearest rest stop. Joshua and Beth discuss the need to safely dispose of the car. Not too far south is a reservoir on Trammel Road. From the earth mapping program, it looks pretty isolated. The short drive to the reservoir gets them to the water's edge slightly after sunset. Joshua loved his car but before sending it to its watery grave, he gently touches the hood to say goodbye.

Goose gently puts its hand on Joshua's shoulder – if a droid could console, maybe this is what it would do. "It's ok Goose – it's just a car I'm not too sad," said Josh.

Goose, "Human display of sadness.

> Webster: Sad: affected with or expression of grief or unhappiness or regret.

What will remove grief, unhappiness, or regret for Joshua Goose? MSA Goose has tools."

Josh, "It's okay Goose, sometimes regret is necessary for humans."

Goose, "**Goose will research regret, thank you Joshua Goose.**"

But Walmart has tools too. It only took two hours for management to realize that the amount of cash dispensed from a scan and go checkout kiosk #4 was an abnormal amount based on customer volume for that time of day. Alerts were sent, surveillance cameras were searched for kiosk 4 during the approximate time of the theft. The camera surveillance showed two adults and a droid. The images appear to be the 'persons of interest' and the credit card used during the purchase is a false number with no identifiable owner. The local police are contacted who immediately contact the FBI.

If Smilin' Sam hadn't been celebrating the $200 cash bonus he'd skimmed from the cash sale of that rattletrap, he might have been at home rather than getting himself a lap dance.

He might have seen the television images of that kid and his sister with the wild red hair earlier today. He might have been able to call that 800FBICRIME phone number to get a reward from them for finding them two kids and the rattletrap van.

By the time he saw the images during supper, the van was already long gone – just like his reward opportunity.

DECOMMISSIONED

RANKIN MEDIA BLITZ

Now that Rankin's researchers in Atlanta knew what to be looking for, they began sending lists of the odd circumstance deaths across the country. The team had been advised to search for emergency room cases of sudden onsets of catastrophic conditions or deaths with no normal morbidity history. The newest reports were showing that previously normally healthy people had been arriving at emergency rooms with a variety of advanced stage symptoms.

The bulk of the reports were coming from hospitals in and around Los Angeles, San Francisco, Houston, Baltimore, Minneapolis, Rochester, Buffalo, and Philadelphia. As these new statistics came pouring into Rankin, he realized that his media blitz was going to need to be national. He was going to need a solution that would sufficiently stimulate the population to get vaccinated in advance of this new lethal virus. So he advised the video production team that they needed to sensationalize the videos. This could be construed as fear-mongering, but considering how lethal the virus was, he felt the embellishment would save lives.

The production is showing video images of children of all races, crying in row upon row of hospital beds. The image now switches to images of mothers rocking their sick and dying children in the streets, crying for their babies. Switching again to images of elderly people not strong enough to walk, coughing and holding their heads, rocking and crying from their suffering from their poor health and that of the dying babies. There are images of nursing staff checking IV bags with tubes running into rows of adult patients. These are the images being prepared for national viewing audiences.

The narrative is running below the pictures of these suffering children and adults, states in large white block letters on a bold red banner, it is narrated by a well-known Hollywood actress. She is choking back the tears as she passionately reads the content of the printed narrative on her teleprompter.

'These children and elderly suffer needlessly across the United States. Why are they suffering and dying from simple childhood diseases that could have been avoided if they had received early childhood vaccinations to protect them? Many of these illnesses came to them from other children at play or in school, some came from the parents and grandparents who never received their own childhood vaccinations or their vaccinations expired. It is SO important for children to get vaccinated immediately – it is just as important for the parents and grandparents to get their booster shots. Save the children, save yourself, call your local health center or physician NOW to schedule your vaccinations. Please for the sake of others, for the sake of the ones you love!'

This video is being shown during every commercial break time on every channel – including every foreign language media channel on television and electronic billboards everywhere.

☐

Every health department, clinic, hospital, and doctor's office has similar posters with the image collages of sick and dying children and old people with bold text emblazoned across the center of the images.

VACCINATION SAVES LIVES – ASK YOUR HEALTH PROVIDER TODAY!

LAS VACUNAS SALVAN VIDAS: ¡PREGUNTE A SU PROVEEDOR DE SALUD HOY MISMO!

IMPFUNGEN RETTEN LEBEN - FRAGEN SIE HEUTE IHREN GESUNDHEITSDIENSTLEISTER!

Yobō sesshu wa inochi o sukuu - anata no kenkō no teikyō-sha ni kyō tazune nasai!

予防接種は命を救う-
あなたの健康の提供者に今日尋ねなさい！

اليوم طبيبك اسأل ، الأرواح تنقذ اللقاحات

The Welfare, Food stamps, and Offices of Public Housing have similar posters on every wall with even more languages in addition to a special poster that declares:

From this date _____forward all recipients must provide proof of vaccination records to continue receiving any and all government benefits. If you have questions, please ask your caseworker who will be happy to provide you a list of providers in your area. Thank you for your cooperation.

NSA/MED/VACC.gov
The NSA in coordination with Bearlywoke Storage had set up a proprietary medical information website with 24x7

online agents. The purpose of this website is to provide the vaccine designation for every person listed by Social Security or drivers' license number. The access channel allows the medical facility (once logged in) to enter the patients' SS number or patient ID to get an immediate response identifying which vaccination is the correct one to be administered for that patient. There are online agents are waiting to research any ID numbers that are not present in the system.

The CDC has issued the official documentation to all medical providers of the criticality of using the NSA/Med/VACC.gov site to ensure that the proper medication is delivered and a web page to obtain the vaccine code for each patient.

* Patient Information

Complete ALL of the following fields to obtain vaccination code

Patient ID:

Name Last:

Name Middle:

Name First:

Date of Birth:

SSN:

Primary Care Physician:

Vaccine to be Administered

Click for Assistance   Done

If the agent cannot identify the proper AVBW# - they are instructed to default to AVBW#D.

The general protocol for these online agents is, if the patient has no social security number, state ID, or established patient ID, the accepted vaccination type will be

AVBW#D (there may be collateral damage, but sometimes shit happens and the support agents have no clue that the #D serum is a death sentence). AVBW#D and AVBW#S are the two most widely administered. The AVBW#G is an optional serum used only for government employees unless the website designates a government employee as AVBW#D.

DECOMMISSIONED

EULESS TEXAS

On the road, Beth asks Goose – "What is SAVIOR Labs, Goose? You are an MSA – I would think you would be used in a hospital, not a Lab."

Goose, binary eye blinking *SAVIOR* = *Security Against Virus in Outbreak Regions* – *SAVIOR*

Goose now vocalizes, "SAVIOR = Security Against Virus in Outbreak Regions. Dr. Ellison D Hampton - decommissioned. MUST SAVE HUMANITY."

This message they had heard before when they first converted the characters, but the "SAVIOR = Security Against Virus in Outbreak Regions" and the part about the decommissioned doctor. These bits of information revealed more clues to their unanswered questions.

It appears, the Doctor was involved in something having to do with viral deaths, and it did sound like this something may have gotten the Doctor killed. But with this small bit of answer, came more questions. For instance, was the doctor part of a foreign activity – or plot against the United States? Was SAVIOR Labs a private laboratory or was it related to the government? The name security implies that the laboratory purpose was meant to protect the USA. Could that be the reason the FBI was involved, that some foreign entity had taken action against a government facility or entity?

☐

Meanwhile

Fire trucks began to arrive shortly after the persons of interest's departure and the fire department broke down the door of the model house with no fire and only a severely smoking scorched table with a medical defibrillator on it

Damn waste of time, two trucks, a broken front door, and someone has to write a report - "What's that a defibrillator? Don't those belong in hospitals?" *Better put that in the report…*Euless fire chief hates doing reports especially when it involved property damaged by his guys and insurance claims that will surely need to be done for this brand new model show house. It's gonna be a long damn night for him.

NSA MONITORING

It has been a bit more interesting today from the normal eavesdropping done in NSA. The earlier red code DOD tracker signal showing up was a bit of excitement that Beau would rather forget ever happened. Beau will probably never know what the follow up was - his job was to monitor and nothing more, there were people above his paygrade to worry about what the content meant. DOD keeps its cards close to the vest. Both Dave Tillis and Beau Clark are thinking about the weekend just a short time away. Dave and Beau are just two in a very large room full of monitor agents, but they've been working together for so long they are more like brothers than co-workers. Both single, they sometimes hang out on weekends to watch a game, and sometimes they talk about what happened that week at work knowing it is against regulations, but it's not like they are telling the world secret stuff. The fact of the matter is that probably very little of what passed in front of their monitor meant very little, but even if the information was pertinent or dangerous material, they probably wouldn't have recognized it as such.

Beau was a Ragin Cajun from the 9th ward of New

Orleans. He rumbled through life with very little incentive to work. He loved food and sports and could have managed to live off the government programs just fine except for the flooding issues down there. Even the government subsidies don't go far when their rental units are filled up with people who used to have jobs. So when a cousin of his, living up in Utah, suggested an opportunity doing support monitoring, he decided he'd take a chance to join the working world.

The pay wasn't so much, but it paid the rent to let him buy food. The work was pretty much, just boring, as he would sit and listen and watch monitors eight hours a day. It wasn't rocket science, but neither was it hard work.

Beau, "Did one of y'all hear something about a missing defibrillator?"

Dave, "Yeah, something why? Whazzup?"

Beau, "I'm seein' a Euliss FD report about a false alarm."

Dave, "Annnnd why do we care about a false fire alarm?"

Beau, "Because there was a stolen defibrillator at the site that has an asset tag on it. Dallas hospital verified it as the stolen equipment from one of their ambulances. FBI is obsessed with a dang defibrillator."

Dave, "CRAP! We better tell someone to get a forensics team there to see if the fire department left any evidence intact. What's the location of the fire?"

Beau made the call because it was his discovery. He thinks, perhaps he will get a reward, a couple of tickets to the game, or a toaster oven.

He contacted his team manager who must follow the chain of command. This can be time-consuming even within a single agency but NSA is a city unto itself. Though the discovery was made at NSA, protocol dictates that the FBI is given the option to act or give permission for another entity to act on an item. From NSA to FBI (Loki) to Carver (FBI) then back to NSA Stephanie Wolff. It's no wonder things slip through the cracks in the government.

NSA assistant to Stephanie Wolff calls to FBI field agents Foote and Mouse – their phones beep simultaneously catching Foote and Mouse in a Dallas Whatta Great Burger joint. What they were discussing was a short list of medical supply locations they would need to check out, in their quest to find a defibrillator.

* * *

Dallas

Test message from Director Wolff, "Stolen defib located 2390 Echo Blvd –Euless TX - FD barricade save forensics" (Euless is 19 miles from Dallas – on nearby Freeway – fast trip from Whatta Great Burger) So Foote and Mouse are quickly on their way to the Euless address.

As Foote and Mouse had feared – the Euless fire department was like a herd of bulls in a china shop – no usable fingerprints but Mouse did find a ponytail rubber band that had some red hairs in it. Bag it, the female person of interest is a redhead in the picture they have plastered everywhere. Maybe the lab can verify it as belonging to the McCallum suspect. They needed to get to the Dallas FBI office to see if anyone checked the defib machine for prints.

No living McCallum relatives – so the lab work on the hair is a bust – but the defibrillator paddles have a couple of vague partial prints that have no value since neither person of interest had a record to match against.

So their race against time out to Euless yielded nothing of value including their cold Whatta Great Burger's. Foote looks at Mouse, "Dang, sometimes we're the windshield, sometimes we're the bug!"

DECOMMISSIONED

DOD

Chuck Delphi calling Ackinsen, "Roger, I've got an incoming call from NSA Stephanie Wolff on the other line. Apparently, the Clearcut tracker is no longer tracking. Do you want me to handle it or do you want to take the call? I was just about to take off for the night....got my Gracie all bot and hothered....so I was gonna bless her with the Delphi charm for a while."

Ackinsen, "What the hell??? Put it through – I don't need this shit. Go ahead and bang that Gracie, don't forget your raincoat, never know what she's been doing. But don't shut your phone off in case I need to get ahold of you later."

Ackinsen picks up the call, "Miss Wolff, how may I help you?"

Stephanie Wolff, "You can help me by explaining how you managed to arm a top-secret Clearcut MSA with an off the shelf P.O.S GPS tracker - with no failsafe backup circuit to ensure that the worlds' most important droid couldn't be compromised! I'd also like to know how much time it will take for you to prepare your resignation if you don't find that droid before some foreign entity does?

I'd also like to know, Mr. Ackinsen, what is your contingency plan if we run out of serum because if you don't get this mess straightened out you are going to wish you had a dose of JMV2030 rather than what I will do to you!"

Ackinsen, "Well good morning to you too, Miss Wolff. If such an accident were to occur, it would fall under the category of collateral damage in a war zone. Since we are at war, indirectly….well, there you have it. I can assure you that I have people on this as we speak, so if you will forgive me, I have other calls waiting for status."

Stephanie Wolff, "48 hours Ackinsen, or I'll personally put your balls in a wringer."

He made a quick call to Chuck Delphi to tell him that Stephanie Wolff was on the warpath over the MSA, but he could handle that Ice Queen Bitch.

DELPHI'S OFFICE DOD

After the brief call from Ackinsen, Chuck Delphi beeps Gracie. "Honey, I need you to get me a secure line to Darla Avery, CIA. Tell them it is about Clearcut and when I'm done with this call – I'm gonna take my favorite hot momma for a treat from Big Dicky Delphi."

Two minutes later, Darla Avery is on the line. "Ok Chuck, what's going on? You know we don't get involved with domestic…"

Delphi, "Darla, honey, it ain't gonna be domestic if Ackinsen isn't removed. I need a favor and you are the only one who can make it happen. We need a pro to remove him and I can't risk any domestic hitter on this."

Darla, "What's the risk if we let him just fall on his sword?"

Delphi, "The risk is a worldwide house of cards coming down on all of us. It doesn't matter what it costs Darla, we are dealing with our power structure here, not just a thinning of one country's population. He's overwhelmed and too much crap is getting loose. I'm not talking about the virus – I'm talking about Clearcut – and our power base."

"He's putting Clearcut at risk? He's done," says Darla.

Chuck Delphi had no clue that 'sweet cheeks Gracie' had been hedging her bets by having a relationship with Travis Loki, nor that she was monitoring and sharing his calls with Travis. *Shit,* thinks Gracie – the thought of Dirty Dicky Delphi's touch made her retch, but personal surveillance was her insurance marker that would provide a way out of here.

MOORE AND TERRY ANGEL

The test results of the samples came back within an hour of Terry's delivery, but the results were not something Joanna felt could be revealed in a phone call to Terry at Bearlywoke. So Joanna was eager to reconnect with Terry.

During their meeting, Terry reveals what she had has found about the AVBW# products which have been escalated in production and distribution to warehouses across the United States and it seems like there have been (yes she confirms) shiploads going to other countries. Joanna has had the AVBW#D, AVBW#G, and AVBW#S tested between Terry's lunchtime drop off and this meeting. The information coming from the laboratory is not good – the #D is not an antivirus at all – but rather it is an active virus with an additional agent that contained the randomized delivery to the recipients. This random delivery explains why Rankin was stymied about the lack of commonality in the death reports.

The #G is an antivirus serum while the #S testing proved to be a placebo. The lists of recipients of the AVBW serums designated the use of all three serums but there was currently no way to know what determined the reason to define who got which serum. There was no other explanation for the naming change to indicate the serum as an anti-virus (AV) when it was, in reality, a deadly active virus, or a useless placebo, in the case of the #S suffix. Joanna realized at this point that the virus must be targeted. Her initial investigation was expected to identify the reason for three different anti-virus agents.

What she had discovered was that the trio of serums included; a useless liquid, an actual anti-virus, and a deadly bio-weapon - and all three of these serums were to be administered to the population of the United States.

Terry is an administrator – but it is clear that what Joanna is telling her that this virus is intended to infect the USA – not protect them – Good God, not just the USA – the entire world!! Yīshēng had said the serums were military bio-weapons – he lied!

Unfortunately, Terry's security authorization had been shut down shortly after her downloading of the Texas population as she began to download the lists of other states.

She provided all the data she was able to get from Bearlywoke records before her security access had been cut off with no warning or explanation. She told Joanna that she doubted if she would even be able to get back into the facility much less into records. She knew she would probably become a fugitive from justice if Yīshēng has shared her action of compromising secret Bearlywoke data.

They agree that they must get to SAVIOR Labs to access Dr. Hampton's records, and get proof of the conspiracy, now revealed by Terry's partial collection of information, identified in the Bearlywoke (DOD) system as Project Clearcut.

Joanna sends Terry ahead because she must quickly try to get ahold of Rankin, he must stop the masses from the continued rush to get the serum vaccinations. She must let Rankin know that the people are rushing to their deaths.

Minutes after Terry's computer is shut down, Art Damone gets a call. The caller has a slight foreign accent, not the same guy who ordered Dr. Hampton. This one said "Terry Angel, Bearlywoke, foreign spy, trying to destroy the USA – Stop her." The caller tells Art that the SAVIOR Labs anti-virus was designed to save the planet from a deadly virus and Terry Angel is a foreign agent who had infiltrated Bearlywoke with the intent of stopping the anti-virus from being distributed to the public. The caller tells him that Bearlywoke discovered her compromising data about the anti-virus distribution process before her access was shut down. The caller expects that her next act will be to try to breach SAVIOR Labs to try to compromise the distribution process.

Art has seen this country dissolving into a world population, escaping the failed ideologies, but wishing to impose these same concepts with the hopes that miraculously, they would work out in this country. The erosion of democracy was seen in all things as the country deteriorated to undisciplined chaos and diminished law and order that had been the things he had solved his whole life.

He believed that the serum was designed to save the country, as reported on the media by the CDC. The job of dispatching the Doctor and taking the damn droid was paid for in full by the government. He has seen the media reports of people rioting to get to the front of the lines in desperate attempts to get the anti-virus.

Now it seems that he has a higher duty – to save a country he loved, it may be that he needed to go rogue... This Terry Angel is going to SAVIOR Labs to destroy the anti-virus distribution process.

DECOMMISSIONED

SAVIOR LABS

In the car, on the way to SAVIOR Labs, Josh and Beth devise their plans to breach the laboratory. They agree it might be safer to separate, so Goose sends a map to the cell phone showing how to find a service entrance. Beth is to drop them at the woody area behind the SAVIOR Labs complex and circle back in 20 minutes. Goose knows its way around the complex, so he and Joshua won't need the map on Beth's phone. The plan is for her to enter the kitchen in 20 minutes allowing Josh and Goose to ensure it is safe inside before her arrival. If Josh and/or Goose are apprehended, they needed to know that Beth was still free to assist.

Beth dropped them off and departed leaving them to breach the fence. There was no time for filleting the chain-link as they had done in recycling ventures. Goose takes charge by cutting the wires and stepping through, but as Joshua stepped through, his human exterior was more vulnerable than that of the metal Goose. A section of razor wire broke loose. Josh was severely cut as the razor wire danced like a cobra when the tension was removed. The deadly sharp wire shot past him, catching his right forearm, tearing flesh, tendons, and nerves. Copious amounts of blood poured forth from severed arteries.

Goose 'has tools' designed to operate medical equipment and for protection, but these tools are not designed for precision medical or surgical procedures. It quickly responded to cauterize the wound to stop the bleeding with no understanding of the traumatic effect the defensive tools may cause when employed to muscles and nerves of that arm.

It didn't understand that though the bleeding was stopped, Joshua would require extensive physical therapy to get those tendons and nerves working properly again. Josh went into mild shock from blood loss and trauma. He was laying on the ground in a pool of his blood, mostly conscious.

Goose easily picked up and carried Joshua through the kitchen door into the lab area to Room #8. This room was a familiar location for Goose and it was also a SKIF – so Goose will be able to collect and transmit data undetected. Beth will be arriving in less than 20 minutes, but this was sufficient time for Goose to upload what it needs and prepare the decommission story for them. Goose knows that if humans are going to help in its mission to save mankind, they will need to understand what has transpired to this point in time.

Joshua is conscious and no longer bleeding, so most of his parts will survive. Goose has tools. If Goose had feelings it would tell the human Joshua, that Goose was remorseful for the injury. Goose had not considered the frail biological body of the human which should have had safer entry access. Goose would like to escort the Beth human safely through the fence if there was time remaining after its priority one item was completed.

Goose still needs circuitry rerouted to be fully functional, but it can download research information from DOD, FBI, and NSA – more importantly, it is downloading from Bearlywoke. Bearlywoke data center was unaware of the changes Dr. Hampton had made. Goose's original programming had been set to transmit data to Bearlywoke.

Doctor Hampton's modifications had redefined so that MSA (Goose) received as well as transmitted to and from Bearlywoke.

When it was time to go get Beth, Goose went to the kitchen but didn't see her. Beth was hiding in the cooler – what Goose found were Foote and Mouse. Foote was about to call for backup – they had discovered the hole in the fence and the blood. Goose was a surprise to them as they had received little intel about the missing droid – they thought they were looking for Josh and Beth (persons of interest in a possible murder). The surprise of encountering Goose was enough for Foote to draw his weapon. "FREEZE!!!" yelled Agent Foote.

Goose employed its tools and tased Foote. Unfortunately for Foote, the controls of many of Goose's systems were out of calibration from the partial decommission. The taser level was on one of the higher settings causing Foote and his phone to fall to the floor. Goose turned toward Mouse. Mouse puts her hands in the air – she doesn't want a taste of Goose's tools.

Mouse, "Woah, woah, woah!!" BUT the phone on the floor is open and she is hoping that the FBI can triangulate on the signal and send backup agents. Goose scanned the area and its heat sensors indicated that Beth was in the cooler, so an exchange was made swapping Beth for Foote. Beth wondered if he would survive until they could return for him.

Meanwhile, Terry had arrived at SAVIOR Labs, but in the main entrance parking lot. She considered what would be the best way to enter the building – hers was not the only vehicle in the lot – but the building seems to have no activity.

Well, she thinks, *I won't know till I try some doors – perhaps it was poor planning to come here without considering how Joanna and I could get inside.*

This was her last thought because as she opened the car door, she received a single lethal shot to the head.

Damone shut the door with his foot and proceeded toward a back entrance. He already knew where the kitchen was located and that it's the easiest entry to the building.

ROOM 8

Goose took both Mouse and Beth to room 8 where Beth begins taping the hands and feet of Agent Mouse. Mouse is about to lose her mind because she knows Foote is injured possibly dying, in a cold locker where Goose had dragged him.

Mouse composes herself enough to tersely address Beth, "You are Beth McCallum – is that right?"

Beth, "Yes I am and we didn't kill the doctor!"

Mouse, "I don't give a shit about the doctor, my friend is injured and you stuck him in the freezer! And if you don't get him out of there and get him some medical attention, I'm going to kill you AND your friend Joshua Klein! I will kill you both, slowly and painfully. I will dismember you both and before you die, I will figure out a way to destroy that fucking robot too!"

Now that Mouse's hands and feet were bound and Goose was standing guard, Beth turned her attention to Josh.

She was horrified to see the condition of Joshua's arm. She carefully checked the condition of the wound and determined that he was neither bleeding nor in shock - he seemed to be returning to the world now. Beth grabbed some paper towels from the counter in an attempt to protect the wound with a makeshift bandage. Beth, "This is gonna have to do until we can get you some proper medical attention. Does it hurt?"

He just looked at her like she had two heads but couldn't find words to respond.

Beth, "Oh – duh on me – of course, it does."

Josh, "You are going to have to help me reroute some of Goose's damaged circuits. "

Beth, "I don't know how to do that Joshua."

Josh, "You have two good hands, I will coach you – you can do this."

Mouse, "What about my partner – he is still in the frickin freezer!!!!"

Beth to Josh, "How long is this going to take?"

Josh, "Between the three of us it should just take a few minutes."

So Josh, Beth, and Goose commence to making the necessary modifications. Partway through the process, Mouse begins to taps her feet on the floor. Beth cast a warning look at Mouse and tells her, "You are not helping the situation…" The warning was sufficient to stop the tapping. A few minutes turned into 10, but they completed the task at hand.

Goose began sharing the story about the killing of Dr. Hampton and the attempted decommission of MSA followed by an account of the human who abducted Goose. The story Included the account of the false story the human had told about Dr. Hampton having suffered a heart attack and the subsequent trip to the warehouse where the RiverMoore human had attempted to decommission Goose. This was the same location where Josh and Beth had found Goose.

MSA was able to project an image of Damone, wearing RiverMoore coveralls, the image clearly shows the fluid leaking from the human's hand. Beth was reminded of the blood she got on herself helping load MSA into the car. Goose finishes with, "`Goose has tools - Must save humanity`"

"Wait Goose", says Beth, "we need to go get Mouse's partner from the kitchen." She then tells Mouse that she will release her to go help get her partner if she will stop impeding their progress. The bit of the story identifies that the country is at risk. Mouse had heard enough to know this is true so she agreed to go with Goose to get Foote, knowing he might need to be carried and that Goose can manage to control her with its tools. Beth stays with Josh in Room 8.

DECOMMISSIONED

THE RETURN TO THE KITCHEN

Goose takes Mouse to the kitchen. They are intending to collect Foote who should have been recovered from being tased. What they find however is Damone, standing over Foote intent on killing him after getting information about where the droid is. It may be that Damone had an order, or perhaps just because he'd had a challenging few days. It may have been that he had gone rogue – and that he believes these people are here to sabotage the effort to save the USA from a deadly virus. The sudden vision of that decommissioned droid set Art into a rage.

Mouse screamed, "NO!"

As Damone turned to shoot the squeaky Mouse, the droid did something to him – he knew not what – but he was suddenly reduced to a shivering hovel of uncontrollable muscles writhing on the floor. Art had been tased before – this was something special and significantly more powerful. It, fortunately, lasted long enough for Mouse to get cuffs on him so Goose could drag him to Room 8 to be re-educated and learn about Project Clearcut.

Suddenly – on the way to Room 8, Goose got Mouse's attention by saying to her, "**SIRENS.**"

CRAP, thought Mouse, Foote had called for backup – Now that she knows the truth the doctor's death – she cannot allow Josh, Beth, and Goose to be apprehended. She tells Goose to get to Room 8 and tell them that she will join them at RiverMoore; she's going to have to wait for the FBI.   Mouse quickly searches Damone for his car keys (which happen to belong to the doctor) and directs Goose and Beth, "Collect up your friend and this guy and get out of here."

Beth, "Where do we go – how are you going to find us?"

Goose to Mouse, "RiverMoore Labs - Goose has friends.   Goose sent a contact to human Mouse phone."

Mouse, "I need to stay with my partner and see to his medical care. Goose, who else do I need to contact?"

Goose, "Bearlywoke Storage. Cool Mann - good. Dr. Yīshēng - human bad."

Mouse to Beth,   "Get the rest of the group into Damone's car and go to RiverMoore Laboratory where someone from RiverMoore will be waiting for them. I will contact someone in charge at that place to wait for you."

Mouse needs to stay with Foote until she can get him some medical transport and divert the search for that team in Room 8. Because Mouse saw the image of Damone while in Room 8, she knows that he might be the murderer of the doctor, but she also knows she can't risk giving him over to the FBI, as she currently doesn't know who he's working for.

Once the FBI and police arrive, she tells them that she and her partner Agent Foote had been about to apprehend McCallum, Klein, and the droid when the droid did something to disable her partner Foote.

She continued explaining that her need to provide aid to her partner provided an opportunity for the three to escape. She yells at the FBI agents to get a medic there quickly and get her partner to the hospital. She will follow in her car and answer any questions they have about McCallum, Klein, and the droid.

The FBI already had people out front investigating the murder in the parking lot, so medical was on the way which would be given priority to Agent Foote. The gunshot victim in the parking lot was gone, there was no saving her.

They quickly took her brief statement and agreed she should follow her partner to the hospital. There is also a need for the FBI and police to investigate the shooting in the front building parking lot. Fortunately for Mouse, their investigation will be a convenient delay for them to arrive at the hospital. This will allow Mouse to insure that Foote doesn't reveal anything he might have seen relating to McCallum and Klein and whoever that other guy is they have cuffed in Room 8.

MOUSE

After the hospital had finished with their triage and Adrian felt safe to move on to other issues, she called RiverMoore. She asked if Joanna had the name of anyone in Bearlywoke who had facilitated Terry because they were going to need someone on the inside due to the extreme security measures at Bearlywoke. Joanna, being a scientist, is used to making notes on everything. Of course, she knew Terry had a contact named Cool Mann who worked in the manufacturing lab at Bearlywoke. Cool had gotten the AVBW samples which Terry had delivered before going to SAVIOR Labs. Adrian recalled the name which the droid had mentioned before they parted ways.

Mouse also had the unfortunate task of telling Joanna that Terry Angel has been murdered. This was very sad news for Joanna – she didn't know Terry really, just a voice on the phone until early yesterday when Terry had delivered the vials of the virus from Bearlywoke. Today the information from Terry may have given Joanna what is needed to save the United States. Joanna realizes that if she had gotten to the SAVIOR Labs to meet Terry there, she may well have ended up dead as Terry now was.

Agent Mouse hangs up and accessed her secure link to government agencies. She isn't top-secret clearance, but before she starts a search she considers – with a name like that – she should be able to find him without tapping secure sites – best to stay under the radar as long as possible. A simple name search gets him easily on social media and she can track him down that way.

Mouse, "Mr. Mann? Are you an employee of Bearlywoke Storage?"

Cool, "Ahhh who wants to know?"

Mouse, "My name is Agent Adrian Mouse from the North Texas division of the FBI."

Cool, "Oh I'm pretty sure you've got the wrong number."

Mouse, "WAIT Cool – don't hang up – Terry Angel is dead!!! If you hang up – you might join her…"

Cool, "Fuck me – my Angel is dead?? She told me there was a conspiracy thing going down; tell me she was in a car accident or something ok? I don't wanna hear she was killed over that virus…"

Mouse, "She was murdered trying to get info about that virus you are making in the lab at Bearlywoke. I need to get you to a safe place so we can figure out a way to stop the distribution of that stuff. Where are you right now? I need to get you before someone bad does. Is your security link still working into Bearlywoke?"

Cool, "Let me check – I have my lap…. Yeah – it's still working. What do you need?"

Mouse, "I need the list of every single distribution center that Bearlywoke has sent that "vaccine' to and any patient name lists you can get. Please make me an SD with the data. Since I was able to find you so easily, we need a meeting place – you need to get away from your home. "

Cool is already downloading the distribution lists in one window and the patient lists in another. He's got a smoking fast laptop, and he tells Mouse to meet him at the

GooeyGood Donut shop on 5th and Main Dallas.

Of course, Mouse knew where GooeyGood was and quickly left to meet him at a Dallas donut shop parking lot where Cool jumps into Mouse's car and off they went to RiverMoore.

RIVERMOORE

Beth drives Damone, Goose, and the damaged Joshua to RiverMoore where Joanna is waiting for them. FBI agent Mouse had called her and told her it was extremely important to protect this team as they have data from SAVIOR that Joanna is going to have to copy and secure. Agent Mouse emphasized the importance of taking extreme measures to protect these four people because there was a breakdown in government. Nobody should be trusted until they can put their heads together and sort this mess out.

Joanna took one look at Joshua's arm and quickly finds the number to call a neurosurgeon friend. She's going to need someone to assess the damage and determine what it's going to take to repair Joshua's arm. Brief introductions are made with the group before Joanna inquires how the injury occurred. Unfortunately, since Beth wasn't present at the time of the accident, she had no clue and Josh was in too much pain to respond – but Goose tells all, "Goose cut fence, Joshua human cut entering fence, losing fluid, Goose has tools. Goose stopped fluid. Help Joshua – recommission Joshua! Must recommission Joshua Goose!"

Joanna tells Goose, "I don't know if Joshua can be repaired Goose."

Goose, "Joshua Goose recommission - yes?" - one blink

Joanna, "Maybe Goose, but now we must stop Clearcut. You did a good thing Goose, you stopped him from bleeding to death."

Goose, "Goose has tools - Must save mankind - Joanna human must recommission Joshua Goose! Joanna human has tools?"

Joanna, "Goose, Joanna human has access to tools. She has ordered tools to come to evaluate Joshua ok?"

Goose, "Ok" – one blink.

Mouse and Cool arrive at RiverMoore and the group of Adrian Mouse, Cool Mann, Joanna Moore, Art Damone, and Beth McCallum now sit and listen to the story of Goose. Joshua Klein is in a clean lab area having his injuries evaluated.

GOOSE

Goose tells them about the human who had abducted Goose up with the story told about Dr. Hampton having suffered a heart attack. The story continued with the description of the following trip to the warehouse including the disabling of MSA's pneumatic system en-route to the recycle location and the subsequent attempt to decommission Goose after arrival at the same recycle location where Josh and Beth had found Goose.

Goose can project an image of Damone, who was wearing RiverMoore coveralls, the image clearly showed the blood pouring from the human's hand. Beth is reminded, once again, of the blood, she had gotten on herself helping load MSA into the car. Beth thinks, *The very person who attempted to decommission Goose is sitting here bound in our presence?*

Agent Mouse is extremely conflicted as she waits for the rest of Goose's story. Her partner Foote is in the hospital in stable condition, but she sure didn't recognize him as the partner she had known and loved for so many years. *His condition was primarily the fault of this nutcase Damone!*

Doctor Hampton had modified Goose – when Goose was commissioned it was programmed to constantly stream the Doctor's research information to Bearlywoke Storage. The streaming data had included the formulae for the vaccine as well as the test results. Contrary to the information that had been given to Rankin, Bearlywoke had a full-scale operation manufacturing, packaging, and distributing truckloads of the vaccine.

Dr. Hampton had decided to make enhancements to Goose's telecommunications. The modification included the ability to receive and record hi-level communications and DOD documents including information about Project Clearcut. Goose did not know the concept of spying or surveillance, but it was programmed to perform these tasks, by Dr. Hampton who did not trust the Bearlywoke organization, for a reason that was beyond MSA's comprehension. MSA was not programmed for emotion or trust.

Now Goose shared the information it had received from Bearlywoke and the truth about the use of JMV2030 including the fact that Bearlywoke is shipping the randomized virus with the intent to disguise its presence as an anti-virus, not what it was in reality, a bio-weapon to be used against the U.S.A.

Art Damone has been listening attentively despite his slightly frazzled brain. He is now filled with fury as he listened to the story that MSA has revealed. The idea that the DOD organization is in the process of killing innocent legal citizens of this country that he loves – that they are waging a biological war against his countrymen, women, and children compromise everything he has believed in his whole life – the sanctity of the government by, of, and for the people.....

Beth tries to talk to Damone. His head is swimming and his emotions are out of control.

Beth, "Look, I know you killed the doctor – I know you tried to decommission Goose. I don't know who you work for or why you killed the doctor, but the FBI thinks Josh and I did this and we have no idea why they think that. We never heard of SAVIOR Labs before or Bearlywoke or RiverMoore either for that matter. Can you explain any of this to me?"

Finally, Art recovers himself enough to speak, "Beth, this is bigger than the doctor – it's bigger than the droid, what we are looking at is the merciless killing of United States citizens. I was hired to do a job, killing the doctor – decommissioning the droid. But it's not a job I'd have taken if I had known it was to kill innocents in my country.

It was suggested that the Doctor was dangerous as if he was some kind of agent – going to sell the "stuff" to another country. I don't know what exactly they said – they just hint at the stuff – contractors don't get much information. It's called 'Need to know...' I just know that it was suggested that doing this job would save my country..."

Beth, "Well you were duped......now we have to find a way to really save the country – are you going to help us or do I need to let Mouse just kill you – she wants to, you know – because you nearly killed her best friend and partner! And if she wants to do that because you won't help us right the wrongs we are seeing in front of us, I will personally stand and watch as she takes her revenge against you. So what do you say? You better tell the truth too, because if you lie, I will know, and believe me when I say - I will let her kill you. Goose is watching, he will know if you tell the truth. So what is it?"

Art, "I will kill any person who puts my country in jeopardy ANYONE up to the president if SHE is involved in this!" He didn't control his breathing – he didn't need to, he was telling the truth.

Beth looked at Goose – one blink.

Beth, "Mr. Damone, you aren't going to kill anyone right now – we need to listen to the story from our Goose."

DECOMMISSIONED

GOOSE'S TALE

Goose, "MSA has prepared the story from databanks, transcribed for human grammar tools. Best displayed on the monitor for human understanding." On the monitor:

I am MSA - DROID – NUMBER MSA121068

Model _ MSA – Medical Studies Assistant

COMMISSION DATE: 6/26/2029

I was in the service of: DR. ELLISON D. HAMPTON, MD – MICROBIOLOGIST, VIROLOGIST SAVIOR Labs (Fort Worth Texas)

My function with Doctor Hampton was ordered by a government team with members from the Department of Defense, the Federal Bureau of investigation, the Central Intelligence Agency, and the United States Army. My programming did not include information regarding the employment of Dr. Hampton but that information was shared by the Doctor with me at a time he deemed appropriate. His research was funded by the same organizations, the DOD, CIA, U.S. Army, with the addition of the National Security Administration (NSA).

The Doctor's primary function was to develop an anti-virus to safeguard the USA military in its use of the biological weapon called JMV2030. He collaborated with members of DOD to determine the need for a modification to the JMV2030 to ensure the virus was not to be recognizable by foreign entities as a bio-weapon but rather for it to appear to be an epidemic of normal viral behavior.

He achieved the function of disguising the bio-weapon by developing and adding a randomizing agent which delayed the onset of the viral agent.

Once the randomizing agent was developed, the Doctor began other projects. He made programming modifications to me. My original programming in addition to that of a regular MSA included a transmit module. The original designated feature was intended to provide a constant stream of data monitoring to be received by a data center within the Bearlywoke Storage (DOD). The doctor, however, when discovering this data stream became concerned about the motives of this feature, so he modified the transmit program to include an algorithm that modified the data to appear diminished or less effective test results which would allow him to expose the true plan for the virus. The other modification he made to me was a receive function that put MSA as a functional constant streaming data collection device to collect communication from the Bearlywoke Storage Data Center.

Shortly after the doctor's testing was complete, Mr. Damone came to tell me the Doctor had a heart attack. I have video images that show Mr. Damone decommissioned Dr. Hampton and attempted to decommission MSA 121068. I would inquire of Mr. Damone the reason for the decommissioning.

At this point, Art Damone opened his mouth to respond, but Beth stopped him by saying, "Goose, you will not employ your tools, Mr. Damone was programmed to do a job - please continue."

Inside MSA 121068 is a data module that is constantly recording all electronic information and activity in Bearlywoke Storage.

Goose, "I will put on the screen the DOD Project Clearcut for your vision. It is a summary of the DOD mission – to destroy a targeted demographic of United States citizens."

PROJECT CLEARCUT
USA - DOD – TOP SECRET
8/14/2027

MISSION PURPOSE: The increase in the population of the United States of America has reached an unsustainable volume resulting in diminished land mass available for purposes of agricultural production. The ratio of working individuals to entitlement subscribers is weighted heavily toward the entitled recipients of government-provided resources.

As the population continues to grow, the USA usable agricultural land availability, and resulting reduced availability of viable food production is disproportionally diminished. The results of the associated statistics are considered by the government to have reached critical mass. The working-class tax dollars are insufficient to finance the purchase of food resources from other countries that still offer commodities for sale.

MISSION SOLUTION: Reduce large numbers of non-participating civilians in the USA

The research model indicates the imminent need to reduce the population of non-contributing residents. The recommendation is to implement a targeted bio-medical solution, for which there is no cure, to quickly eliminate the drain on the country's resources. Analogous to the deactivation of an older model droid, we will refer to this necessary purging of non-contributing humans as Human Viral Decommissioning (HDV).

MISSION IMPLEMENTATION:

DOD and the US Army control the facility known as RiverMoore Laboratories. RiverMoore is a primary research and storage location of biological weaponry, virus, and bacterial research projects. RiverMoore laboratories will be commissioned to manufacture a biological weapon for the Army. Their security status will preclude them from the knowledge of the Primary Mission of this viral bio-weapon.

RiverMoore Laboratories will also be in charge of subcontracting the research and development of a vaccine intended for the list of intended protected governmental and designated civilians targeted for protection.

DOD will be a principal financier of the subcontracted vaccine research to ensure the security of the vaccine's limited distribution. Subcontractor lab (Security Against Virus in Outbreak Regions) SAVIOR LABS will, as with RiverMoore, be precluded from the knowledge of the intended distribution of the anti-viral vaccine and possible reagent.

SAVIOR LABS will be equipped with a state of the art MSA model android to assist in research with its primary goal being the maintenance of all records of research and development activity. This information will be automatically backed up remotely to data storage at the DOD Bearlywoke facility. MSA model droid will be custom designed and equipped with a nuclear power supply and GPS tracking capability until such time that it is decommissioned. DOD will also coordinate with the US Army for enhanced military defenses and assistance features built into the MSA model android for its protection.

IMPLEMENTATION TARGET GOAL: 6/14/2028
MISSION TARGET GOAL REACHED: 9/11/2029

DECOMMISSIONED

EPILOGUE

Emmett Rankin (CDC) has been watching the news coverage. Riotous masses trying to penetrate the lines of people who have been standing for hours to get their anti-virus vaccinations – The media blitz was professionally done and it hit its mark as the population attempted to save themselves from the CDC projected epidemic (just as Delphi had planned).

In between the video clips of riots and lines of people is the occasional brief coverage of a Washington, DC incident where a car explosion is reported. Early in the morning, a DC neighborhood was rocked by the explosion. The car is believed to belong to Roger Ackinsen, Director of the Department of Defense. Fire officials report that they have not ascertained the cause of the explosion. They further state that there was a single body in the vehicle but forensics have not yet verified the name of the driver/victim – whether it was Mr. Ackinsen or his driver. The news reporter adds that the whereabouts of Mr. Ackinsen is currently unknown. The cause of the explosion has not been determined, but terrorism has not been ruled out.

Charles Delphi has assumed the role of Acting Director of Department of Defense until such time that Mr. Ackinsen is established as dead in the fiery explosion of his car.

Joanna Moore watches round the clock the news coverage of chaos in the streets as the people stampede to get to the front of the lines to receive what they believe to be anti-virus.

Unbeknownst to Rankin is that his media blitz, to get the people to the lines to get vaccinated are translated into many languages for use around the world. Neither did he know that the other countries of the world had distribution centers waiting for the global distribution orders from top world powers.

Yīshēng Sǐwáng smiles as he pushes the "SEND' button on the email that initiates the distribution order to begin in his and other Asia Pacific regions to begin the World Clearcut Project. His private jet pilot is waiting on the tarmac for the control tower clearance to take-off. The doctor won't be returning to the USA – he has work to do in China. Then the real power will be in his grasp.

Joshua is receiving physical therapy for the damaged arm as Beth downloads the terabytes of information from Goose that will need to be compiled and shared with some authority that is not associated with the Clearcut Project. They are now part of a small group with a mission to stop the genocide. They are Savior Unit.

DECOMMISSIONED

COMING ATTRACTIONS

Watch for these, soon to be published books, by Maryellen:

SAVIOR UNIT - THE SEQUEL TO
DECOMMISSIONED (DEC. 2020)

Clearcut was a planned distribution of a biological weapon to radically reduce large numbers of the population within select target groups while saving those contributors to the tax system and specific political voting blocks. The launch of Clearcut returned reports of extraordinary success.

The number of deaths was staggering and DComm Group was pleased.

There are some, however, not part of DComm, who know the truth of Project Clearcut. This small team is committed to finding a way to stop Project Clearcut. Their goal is to save the population of the United States and remove the corruption existing in the present administration. They worked undercover, risking their lives to collect the proof of the genocide and to recruit an army of patriots intent upon regaining the freedom of the United States.

Their mission is to save the population and restore the United States of America to its original democratic republic, this group is growing, they are Savior Unit...........

IOTAA – published by Fulton Books

They came in peace from the furthest reaches of the universe and brought with them the knowledge and technology to defeat the time and distances that had for a millennium, shackled the inhabitants of Earth to the confines of a single planet.

In collaboration with the scientists of Earth, they built the technological systems for intergalactic travel. There were many earth-class planets scattered throughout the universe, each with its unique environment waiting patiently to host visiting lifeforms.

From the efforts of many, the Intergalactic Operational Transport Authority Agency (IOTAA) was spawned to facilitate the new cooperative sharing of interplanetary opportunities.

IOTAA is a story of survival, corruption, greed, adversity, adventure, intrigue, competition, and fantasy – wrapped up, marketed and tied up with a bow of irony.

IOTAA IS A STORY THAT WILL NEVER BE FORGOTTEN.

Notes from the author

At the time Decommissioned was written, there was no real-world Covid-19 pandemic. This story was written purely as science fiction. Though the fictional virus of this story is different in some ways, from the present worldwide pandemic, the similarities, parallels, and possibilities continue to be staggering......The prophetic behavior of the fictional virus in Decommissioned has not been edited to reflect the behavior of the 2020 Covid-19 Novel Corona Virus.

ABOUT THE AUTHOR

A big-city girl living in small-town Idaho, Maryellen Hunter
is an avid reader turned writer with a newfound passion for
science fiction. Her life's travels and experiences combined
with the joy of meeting and conversing with people of all
types provide the seeds to create unique characters and
situations. With her first book – Decommissioned – she
sets her vivid imagination and experiences into words to
share with others as she weaves a tale of conspiracy and
deceit with unlikely heroes - to paint the pictures of people,
places, and events for her reader's enjoyment.